Jessica Darling's ★IT★ LIST

THE (totally not) GUARANTEED GUIDE to POPULARITY, PRETTINESS & PERFECTION

A NOVEL BY MEGAN MCCAFFERTY

poppy

LITTLE, BROWN AND COMPANY
New York   Boston

Copyright © 2013 by Megan McCafferty
Excerpt from *Jessica Darling's It List 2* copyright © 2014 by Megan McCafferty

Poppy

Hachette Book Group
237 Park Avenue, New York, NY 10017
Visit our website at lb-kids.com

Poppy is an imprint of Little, Brown and Company.
The Poppy name and logo are trademarks of Hachette Book Group, Inc.

The publisher is not responsible for websites (or their content) that are not owned by the publisher.

First Paperback Edition: August 2014
First published in hardcover in September 2013 by Little, Brown and Company

Library of Congress Cataloging-in-Publication Data

McCafferty, Megan.
   The (totally not) guaranteed guide to popularity, prettiness & perfection /
Megan McCafferty.—First edition.
      pages cm.—(Jessica Darling's it list)
   Summary: The day before seventh grade begins, twelve-year-old Jessica Darling
gets a list from her sister, whose popularity and beauty made her a junior-high
standout, but when she tries to follow it, all goes awry, including losing her
best friend.
   ISBN 978-0-316-24499-2 (hc) — ISBN 978-0-316-24498-5 (pb) —
ISBN 978-0-316-24497-8 (ebook)
   [1. Junior high schools—Fiction.   2. Schools—Fiction.   3. Popularity—
Fiction.   4. Individuality—Fiction.   5. Best friends—Fiction.   6. Friendship—
Fiction.   7. Sisters—Fiction.   8. Family life—Fiction.]   I. Title.
   PZ7.M47833742Tot 2013
   [Fic]—dc23

                                                                    2012048545

10 9 8 7 6 5 4 3 2 1

RRD-C

Printed in the United States of America

For the ladies of Littlebrook

Chapter One

What happens when EVERYTHING you know about ANYTHING is ALL WRONG?

That's what I'm about to find out.

Today is the last day of summer. I'm supposed to start seventh grade tomorrow. I say "supposed" to start seventh grade because I don't know if I can show up for my first day so tragically unprepared for Pineville Junior High.

My sister would say otherwise. She'd argue that I'm way better off now than I was before I received her big sisterly wisdom. She promises that if I follow her must-do IT List I won't merely survive junior high—I'll *thrive.*

And she would know better than anyone what it takes to make it in seventh grade. Ten years ago Bethany Darling was the IT Girl at Pineville Junior High School. All the boys wanted to date her and all the girls wanted to be her. I was only a baby at the time, but I've seen the pictures and I swear her life was as perfect as a shampoo commercial.

My life isn't like a shampoo commercial. But don't feel bad for me because it isn't like the educational films about bullying that we're forced to watch during Be Kind to Each Other week at school either. I have plenty of friends. And until my sister gave me the IT List, my best friend, Bridget, was the one freaking out about starting junior high—not me. I guess if I had to describe myself, I'd say I'm very witty, medium pretty, and a little bit zitty. I'm not the worst off but there's definitely room for improvement.

So when Bethany surprised me this morning by taking time out of her busy social schedule to give me life-changing advice before my first day of seventh grade, I wasn't exactly in a position to refuse. Besides, Bridget is in a state of total discombobulation about junior high. I figured I could share any valuable information that could help her, uh, *re*combobulate. If such a thing is even possible.

"It must be so hard to have your big sister away at college during such an important time in your life," Bethany said with a cluck of her tongue and a sympathetic shake of her head.

Despite my best efforts, my sister and I have never really been that close. That's what happens when you're born in different decades. When she was my age, I was still wetting my pants. That will put a wedge in any relationship. I've always admired my sister from afar in the same sort of way Bridget looks up to certain celebrities. We see the teensiest bit of ourselves in our idols, but their lives are so glamorously out of touch with our boring reality.

"The transition from elementary school to junior high school can't be taken lightly," Bethany continued. "The choices you make during the next two years directly affect your popularity in high school, which directly affects your popularity in college, which directly affects what sorority you get into, which directly affects who you meet and who you marry, which directly affects your popularity every day thereafter until you *die*."

Bethany paused just long enough for the seriousness of her speech to sink in.

"Choices. So many choices."

Then she dramatically took me by the shoulders.

"So many chances to make *so! many! mistakes!*"

I'm not exaggerating when I say a shiver shot up my spine when she said that and not just because she grabbed me so hard my back was thrown out of whack.

"And that's why I'm going to share my wisdom with you, my little sister."

Then she patted me on the head, which was kind of

funny because I'm already as tall as she is and she had to reach up to do it. Then, with the grace of a professional game show hostess, she reached into her designer handbag and pulled out a three-by-five card. She teasingly dangled the small piece of paper in front of my grabby fingers before finally letting me have it.

Here! In my hands! The sacred document containing all the secrets to a lifetime of awesomeness! I thought.

Until I actually looked at it.

"Uh, your old Pineville Junior High Cheer Team travel schedule?"

"The life-changing advice is on the back," Bethany said with a deep sigh, as if this were the most obvious thing in the world.

And when I *did* the most obvious thing in the world—flip it over to see the life-changing advice for myself—she slapped my hand away.

"Not now!"

"Ow!" I cried, rubbing my stinging wrist. "Why not now?"

"You need to take in this life-changing advice all on your own, without me there to spell it out for you." She spoke sagely. "That's part of the process."

I stared down at the card in my hand. What sort of life-changing advice could be on the flip side of a decade-old Pineville Junior High Cheer Team travel schedule? How much could there possibly be to spell out? There's barely enough room to spell out G-O, J-E-S-S-I-C-A!

My sister pulled a pouty face.

"Why am I not being embraced with gratitude right now? Why am I not being celebrated as the most awesome big sister of all time? Why am I feeling like the recipient of this great life-changing advice does not appreciate the gift I have given her?"

"Thank you, Bethany. Seriously. But..."

Bethany checked the time, already more concerned about leaving than actually being here.

"Hey, has the mail arrived yet?" she asked.

And before I could say yes, she was already at the front door, elbow deep in the mailbox. She rifled through the catalogs, bills, and miscellaneous junk, sighed, and then put the whole stack back.

"Are you looking for something?" I asked.

"No!" she yelped. "I mean, yes!" She relaxed and pinched my cheek. "I mean, mind your own business, Little Miss Seventh Grader!"

Bethany gets all jumpy when she's in Pineville for too long, and I could tell she was beyond eager to head back to campus before my parents even realized she was home. Bethany loves college so much that she's taking a fifth year to graduate.

"I just can't imagine how whatever is on the back of this card is going to change my life."

Bethany tossed all her blond hair over from one shoulder to the other.

"Are you questioning my authority? I was voted Most Popular, Prettiest, and Miss Perfect in the Pineville Junior High yearbook. If I'm not an expert on such matters, then who is?"

She had a point there. I followed her off the front porch, followed her down the driveway, and followed her to her boyfriend's convertible. At that moment I would've followed her anywhere. Bethany has that effect on people. If I follow her rules, will *I* have that effect on people? Is that what it means to be popular?

"Didn't you keep a diary that, I don't know, explains *how…*"

My sister cut me off with knowing laughter.

"Popular girls don't keep diaries, because they're too busy being popular to write about being popular," she said, opening the car door and sliding inside. "Which is a shame because popular girls are the ones with juicy stuff worth reading."

I'd actually considered buying a diary to document the momentous occasion that was the start of seventh grade. Bethany just saved me $1.99.

"Just follow my advice and remember who you are," Bethany said with familiar finality as she fluffed her hair in the rearview mirror. "You're a Darling."

"I'm a Darling," I repeated.

"Darlings aren't dorks!"

Then Bethany slipped on a pair of dark sunglasses and backed out of the driveway.

The irony is this: I wasn't at all worried about being a seventh-grade dork until my sister said that.

Chapter Two

Bethany Darling's IT List
The Guaranteed Guide to Popularity,
Prettiness & Perfection

1. Wear something different every day.
2. Make the CHEER TEAM!!!
3. Pick your first boyfriend wisely.
4. Stick with the IT clique.

That's it.

That's *IT*?

Twenty words (I'm counting "!!!" as its own word) written on the back of a Pineville Junior High CHEER TEAM!!! travel schedule in smudged scarlet lip liner? It reminded me of Bridget's disastrous eyebrow-plucking tutorial: so simple and yet totally impossible to follow without scarring myself in some permanent way.

I only had about ten seconds to wrap (warp?) my brain around the IT List before I heard my best friend's footsteps kicking up gravel in our driveway. I quickly hid the old schedule inside a copy of *The Outsiders*. That's the novel the entire incoming seventh grade was supposed to read over the summer. I'd already read it once, but I wanted it to be fresh in my head. I've heard that teachers give quizzes on the first day of school to find out right away who's a star and who's a slacker. I bet there won't be any slackers in the seventh-grade Gifted & Talented classes, though. You don't get into G&T by being a slacker.

Anyway, *The Outsiders* is set in the 1960s and it's all about cool versus uncool kids, which goes to show you that people have been preoccupied with popularity since the olden days, an idea that has already taken on whole new significance in my life since my sister decided to TOTALLY MESS WITH MY HEAD ON THE LAST DAY OF SUMMER BEFORE I START SEVENTH GRADE.

This was also Bridget's last day to freak out about starting seventh grade and she was going to make the most of it. Her pale skin screams red when she's under emotional duress so she came careening across the yard like a fidgety zinnia in full-bloom freak-out. She barreled through the pleasantries and got right down to business.

"Is it too late for you to change your last name?" she asked.

Did Bridget eavesdrop on the conversation with my sister from across the street? Bethany's voice was loud and clear in my ears.

You're a Darling. Darlings aren't dorks!

Bridget nervously braided and unbraided her waist-length white-blond hair as she babbled on.

"I was thinking that you could change it to something that starts with the letter *M* so we can at least be in the same homeroom!"

Whew. Bridget hadn't overheard my sister after all.

"Jessica *Marling* has a nice ring to it!"

The thing about Bridget is that I've known her my entire life and I still can never be sure when she's kidding or not.

"Why don't *you* change *your* last name?" I asked.

Bridget's last name—Milhokovich—is never pronounced correctly. Bridget has heard it so many ways (Mill-HOCK-O-vitch, Meel-HOE-KOE-vitch, Mill-HOCK-O-LOOGIE) that she answers to all of them. I'm not sure she even knows the right way to say it anymore.

"My mom just got this monogrammed for me."

She pulled her backpack off her shoulder and thrust it

in my face for inspection: *BMB* embroidered in pale pink on hot pink canvas.

"Sooooo...what do you think? New school, new name, new you!"

Bridget grinned hopefully, and I pretended to be blinded by sunlight bouncing off her braces.

"SHUT MOUTH. TOO BRIGHT."

I rolled myself into a ball to shield myself from the killer orthodontic glare. She retaliated by kicking me in the butt. It was all silliness for a few seconds before Bridget got dead serious.

"What if we don't have any classes together, Jess?" she worried. "I wish I wasn't so stupid!"

"Bridget!" I protested for the bazillionth time. "You aren't stupid!"

"Fine," she settled. "I'm not stupid. But I'm two points shy of Gifted and Talented and that's enough to keep me out of all your classes."

Sigh.

Bridget and I both took the entrance exam that determines which students get accepted into Pineville Junior High's Gifted & Talented program. I got in. Unfortunately Bridget missed the cutoff by two points. Two points! Mrs. Milhokovich called the school hoping they'd make an exception, but the spaces are limited so, no.

That two-point deficit was one of the biggest reasons why Bridget was freaked out about seventh grade.

I've tried not to be too bummed about it because I've never had problems making friends and that's kind of the point of junior high, right? To make new friends and keep the old? Isn't that what I learned in Girl Scouts before I was asked to leave the organization because one too many orders of Thin Mints were delivered with a poorly taped-up box top and a missing cookie sleeve?

(In my defense: Thin Mints are delicious and my mom is always on a diet.)

"What if no one talks to me?" Bridget worried. "Who will I talk to?"

When I heard that tiny voice, I knew it wasn't time for messing around anymore. Plus her whole body was like a sunburn, even though she had joined me in the safe shade of our oak tree. I wasn't so psyched about tomorrow either, but Bridget was my best friend and I was determined to make her feel better.

Unfortunately, this wasn't a role I was born to play. Bridget was the natural cheerer-upper, not me. Even back in our Pack 'n Play days my mom says that Bridget would offer me her pacifier, her sippy cup, even her beloved stuffed octopus when I was cranky and crying for no apparent reason. I always took whatever she was offering and calmed down. This is pretty much the way our twelve-year friendship has always worked.

There's really only been one time in her life when it was my turn to make her feel better. It was a bit disturbing that starting seventh grade seemed to upset Bridget almost as much as her parents' divorce three years ago. But I had helped her through that, so I could get her through this.

Right?

"I'll talk to you," I promised. "We'll see each other every morning on the bus to school and every afternoon on the bus home."

Bridget smiled, her face cooling to a light pink that matched the *BMB* embroidered on her backpack. It was working. *I* was making *her* feel better for a change.

"We'll always live across the street from each other, Bridge," I said. "You can show up at my house uninvited anytime you want."

And then I kicked her in the butt just to show her how much I really cared.

Chapter Three

Sufficiently un-freaked-out, Bridget spent the next half hour presenting me with photos of her first-day-of-school fashion options.

We were in my dad's office, otherwise known as the Techno Dojo. Whatever the latest bleep-blooping gadget there is to have, my dad has it. He's baffled by my indifference to all things technological. He gets paid to fix computer problems all day, but I swear he would totally do it for free. I think Dad prefers computers to people.

Anyway, Bridget was bleep-blooping in front of the largest screen, all the better for side-by-side critiques of mix-and-match combinations of hairstyles, tops, bottoms, and footwear.

"So I'm pretty sure I'm almost, like, one hundred

percent-ish decided that I think I've narrowed it down to these four hairstyles, these four tops, these four bottoms, and these four pairs of shoes!"

I didn't have the heart to tell her that math was against her: Just those items alone gave her 256 options. And if accessories were involved, her choices could easily run into the thousands.

She hadn't bothered asking me what I was going to wear because I pretty much have one look: a T-shirt and jeans. Mom took me shopping at the mall and after a "tempestuous debate" (her words) and a "major blowout" (my words) regarding a certain flowered skirt that was "so adorable" (her words) and "so gagtastic" (my words), we came home with a fresh supply of T-shirts and jeans in Mom-approved colors and patterns. That I'm not a fashion person is a great mystery and disappointment to my mother. Anyway, we all assumed my first-day-of-seventh-grade outfit would invariably involve a T-shirt and jeans.

That is, until I remembered #1 on the IT List.

1. Wear something different every day.

Nothing in my closet qualifies as "something different." Everything I own is from the mall. Sameness is the whole point of buying stuff at the mall. You buy stuff at the mall knowing that lots of other girls will buy the same stuff at the mall so you won't be ostracized for dressing like a freakazoid. Why would my sister encourage me to wear "something different" unless that uniqueness would have a positive impact on my popularity? Was she actually encouraging me to stand out instead of blend in?

That didn't sound like the Bethany I knew. At all. But she was the undisputed queen of junior high and I most definitely am not.

"Jess! Are you even listening to me?"

"Of course I'm listening," I lied. "That's it! Hair half-up, half-down. Striped top. Capris. Slip-ons. Awesome."

That must have been the right thing to say because Bridget blew out a huge sigh of relief. Well, at least *one* of us had solved our first-day-of-seventh-grade wardrobe crisis. I was about two seconds away from blabbing to Bridget about the IT List and the possible negative repercussions of my unimaginative closet when my parents' car honked for my attention.

"Yikes," I said with a groan. "You better get out of here or they'll make you help put away the groceries."

They would, too. Bridget spends so much time at my house that my parents treat her as annoyingly as they do their own flesh and blood. Only Bridget doesn't think my parents are the least bit annoying. She says I should appreciate how lucky I am to have two parents around to annoy me all the time. I shut my mouth when she says that, as I usually do whenever Bridget so much as hints at her parents' split, which isn't very often because she doesn't want to bum everyone out. My parents just love Bridget's positive personality and ever-pleasant disposition, and pointing this out to me just happens to be another one of the annoying things they do.

"Oh! I have to get home, anyway," Bridget said as she scooped up her backpack.

Bridget flashed a particularly tinny grin and waved at my parents through the open window. Honestly, she's always as happy to see them as they are to see her.

"Today's such an important day!" she shouted to my parents.

"It *is* an important day!" Mom called out in agreement. "So much to do!"

"The last day before seventh grade," Dad announced unnecessarily, the way dads who don't know how to talk to kids tend to do.

I watched Bridget skip back across the street to her house. She seemed oddly carefree for someone who was so stressed out just moments before. I guess I'm pretty good at being the supportive friend after all.

"Help your mother with the groceries, Notso!"

Notso is what my dad calls me, as in Jessica "Notso" Darling. Ha-ha. I pretend to hate it, but it kind of suits me, to tell you the truth. Darling really is a tough name to live up to, more than ever since Bethany shared the IT List. Never before had I been so tempted to change it to something a little less cutesy: Jessica Disappointing. Jessica Duh. Jessica Dork.

"Come on," Mom coaxed. "Most of this stuff is for you."

I was actually grateful for an excuse not to obsess over the IT List. But I dragged my feet just long enough to make my parents think that helping them was, like, the hugest inconvenience of my life. You can't let parents think they can bother you to do stuff whenever they want or they'll start bothering you to do stuff whenever they want.

Which they already do anyway, now that I think of it.

Chapter Four

For someone who makes a point not to eat very much, Mom was very excited about all the back-to-school food.

"I didn't get the chocolate chip cookies you asked for, but I did get these *wonderful* cranberry granola bars. And I didn't get the sugary cereal you asked for, but I did get these *delightful* Flax Flakes. And I didn't get the soda you asked for, but I did get this *flavorful* seltzer...."

The rest of the unpacking went exactly like that: "ful" of crappy food I didn't ask for and didn't want.

"You just missed Bethany this morning," I said, wincing at the stinky Brie that must have been a substitute for the Cheddary-product-in-a-can I'd requested.

My mother almost dropped an economy box of organic green tea bags on her tennis shoes.

"Bethany was here? Didn't her classes begin weeks ago? Shouldn't she be in class? Where's she getting the money to pay for gas to cruise around town without a care in the world? Why wouldn't she tell me or your father? Why didn't she stay?"

Gee, Mom. I have no idea why she wouldn't want to stick around for one of your classic interrogations.

Dad entered the kitchen with the last of the groceries.

"Dar!" That's what she calls my dad. It's short for Darling, obviously, but to me it sounds like the name for a caveman. "Dar! Bethany was here this morning!"

My father almost dropped a bag of produce on his cycling shoes.

"Bethany was here? Didn't she start classes a few weeks ago? Shouldn't she be in class? Where's she getting the gas money to go on joyrides? Why wouldn't she tell us? Why didn't she stay?"

Say what you want about my parents. Call them dorky and uptight, clueless and pushy. (I do.) But they are meant for each other.

They both turned to me for answers. For a split second I was tempted to mention how she'd spied through the mail, but I thought better of it. My sister's business was none of my business.

"She came to see me. To offer me, you know, big sisterly life-changing advice before starting school."

My dad barked a laugh and muttered, "Maybe you should offer her little-sisterly life-changing advice about *finishing* school."

My mom got a wounded look and swatted him on the shoulder with a supermarket circular.

"She changed her major, Dar. You can't expect her to graduate in four years if she changed her major."

My mom always defends Bethany. Fortunately, my dad usually sides with me. I think these allegiances are based on appearances.

Mom and Bethany are both blond and blue-eyed, petite yet curvy in the way that looks just right to me, but they are always complaining is too fat. Mom says she has to look good because her picture appears on real estate signs in front yards all over Ocean County. She says it's an "occupational hazard," but that doesn't explain why Bethany worries about her looks even more than Mom does, because my sister doesn't have a job. If my mom and my sister are any indication, it seems to me that the prettier you are, the more you worry about how pretty you are, which doesn't make any sense at all.

Maybe that's because I look more like my dad. We're dark-haired (or what's left of my dad's hair is, anyway) and brown-eyed, with skinny arms and legs attached at awkward angles to our gangly bodies. Prettiness is not something I spend a lot of time thinking about because I'm too busy thinking about other things. Thinking about things is my primary hobby. As hobbies go, it's kind of a weird one. Thinking about things isn't like taking dance classes or playing soccer or crafting or something normal like that. People can go to a performance or cheer at a game or ooh and ahh over a birdhouse made of Popsicle sticks or whatever. But when thinking about things is your hobby, there's nothing to show for it. No "Hey, take a look at all the stuff going on inside my brain!" So whenever someone asks what I like to do in my free time—and that someone is usually a grown-up because it's exactly the kind of question grown-ups love to ask—it's just way easier to say that I like to read because I can direct them to all the books on my shelves.

Obviously, this is something I've thought about. A lot.

So what other kinds of things do I think about? It's hard to say. I think about whatever pops into my head and it's very hard to stop thinking about it as soon as it does. There are two categories of thinking: Deep Stuff and Dumb Stuff.

Like, the other morning I woke up wondering about all the background people who are in my dreams. I'm talking about the people I don't know or recognize from real life. Am I making those people up or do they really exist somewhere? Are they people I might have seen one time in my life, like, at the mall, but my brain captured their images and held on to them just to use them later as extras in my dreams? Or are they people who exist somewhere in the world who I haven't ever seen or met, but we're connected through some deeper human consciousness?

That's a pretty good example of Deep Stuff.

And then there's the Dumb Stuff, like when I spent an hour ranking my favorite ice-cream flavors (#1: Cookie dough).

My dad is a thinker, too. Stress sweat was just starting to shine on his balding head.

"Did Bethany have to wait until second semester of her junior year to change her major? And from Public Relations to Image Marketing and Management? I don't get the difference. You're good with words, Notso. Do you understand the difference between Public Relations and Image Marketing and Management?"

I did NOT understand the difference between Public Relations and Image Marketing and Management, which is why I immediately excused myself to the privacy of my bedroom to figure it out.

And by that, I mean I called Bethany.

Chapter Five

I knew my sister had asked me not to seek deeper clarification of her life-changing advice because I had been specifically instructed that the struggle was part of the process. But at least ninety minutes had passed since we'd last spoken, so I figured she wouldn't think I was pestering her unnecessarily.

I was wrong.

"Please do not tell me that you are already seeking deeper clarification on my life-changing advice when I specifically instructed you that the struggle was part of the process," she said instead of saying hello.

"Uh," I stammered. "It's just that, well, I'm already kind of confused about the first one, you know, about wearing something different...."

She sighed so loud that I bet I could have heard her clear across the state of New Jersey even without the phone.

"I am a very busy girl," she began. "It's so hard juggling an active social life, an active love life, an active philanthropic life as part of the sorority sisterhood…"

"And your academic life?" I added. "Your classes?"

"Yeah, sure, whatever," she said breezily. "Anyhoo, you'll figure out how to use the IT List to your greatest advantage. Trust yourself."

Trust myself. Yikes. I thought I could trust how to handle myself in junior high UNTIL SHE TOTALLY MESSED WITH MY HEAD.

"More important, trust *me*."

Trust her. If I can't trust my own sister, who can I trust? It's never been my ambition in life to be popular, but at the very least I can try to uphold my sister's legacy by not being a total dork. Bethany of all people wouldn't encourage me to do anything to dorkify the Darling name, right?

RIGHT?

"*I'll* check in with *you* at appropriate intervals," she promised. "Until then, consult my closet for inspiration. Oh! And tell Mom and Dad they need to deposit more money in my checking account to buy, uh, books and stuff. Okaythanksbye!"

With that, my big sister left fate up to me.

And her closet.

Her closet! Which is in her bedroom!

Bethany's bedroom is right next to mine, but it might as well be on the other side of the planet. Bethany has always been very particular about protecting her privacy. My whole life I was warned NEVER TO SET FOOT IN HER ROOM. When she was my age, she actually paid a neighborhood nerd to design and install a baby booby trap involving a laundry basket, bungee cords, and a talking teddy bear. By the time I was a toddler I knew well enough to KEEP OUT OR DIE. This rule stands even now that she's away at college, not that she still openly threatens me or anything. It's just habit. Or survival instinct.

Being granted permission to access her closet was, like, totally unprecedented. This made me all queasy with excitement and trepidation because it spoke to the magnitude of importance Bethany placed on starting off junior high the *right way* and my strict obedience to the IT List in particular. Even so, I was, perhaps, overly cautious about opening the door to Bethany's room. I hesitated with my hand hovering over the doorknob because, okay, I was paranoid Bethany was testing me somehow and that her room might be rigged with an invisible magnetic fence system like the kind that prevents your dog from peeing on the flower beds.

I might still be wimping out in the hallway if my parents hadn't unintentionally intervened.

"Help your mother with the laundry, Notso!"

"Most of this stuff is for you!"

Bethany's room was the last place they'd think to look for me. I grabbed the knob, flung open the door, and slipped inside. I was safe from sorting whites from darks for the time being.

Bethany's room was decorated with a lot of pictures of...Bethany. Bethany in her CHEER TEAM!!! uniform, Bethany as Homecoming queen, Bethany chugging out of a big red plastic cup, Bethany in a sorority sweatshirt. There were other girls and boys surrounding her in the pictures, too, but the focal point of every photo was always Bethany, Bethany, and more Bethany.

Bethany is very pretty. Have I mentioned that? And the pictures with all her many male and female friends indicate that she is also popular. And therefore—according to the indisputable experts on yearbook committees—perfect.

Even though she hadn't slept here in a week the room still smelled like her—a powdery, flowery perfume mixed with something chemical. Maybe her Bombshell Blond hair dye? ("Highlights!" she'd protest.) I wondered if my room had a signature scent. If it did, it probably smelled like contraband chocolate chip cookies, Cap'n Crunch, and Coke.

Anyway, Bethany's room was otherwise beige and very boring. It was a huge letdown, really, like waiting in line for two hours for a roller-coaster ride that lasts ten seconds and sucks for nine of them.

I had to stay focused.

Consult my closet for inspiration.

The closet! I'd learn everything I needed to know about dressing the right way for junior high by looking inside this closet.

I opened the closet doors and...

COLORS! SO MANY! TOO MANY! COLORS! BLINDING! COLORS! And MORE COLORS! And PATTERNS! PLAIDS! FLOWERS! STRIPES! POLKA DOTS! SQUIGGLY THINGIES I THINK ARE CALLED PAISLEY!

Bethany's closet was about a bazillion times crazier than the rest of her blah bedroom. *Consult my closet for inspiration.* Inspiration? Ha! I'd need anti-nausea medication.

I took a deep breath and struggled to push the clothes-heavy hangers from one side to the other, hoping that one item—a purple satin tuxedo jacket, a rainbow-striped maxi dress—would finally present itself as the perfectly "different" thing for me to wear on my first day of seventh grade. I slowly made my way from front to back, left to right. After more than an hour of searching, I couldn't possibly imagine myself wearing any of it! I slumped to the floor of the closet in fatigue and frustration.

"Why won't you just tell me what to do?!" I shouted at a photo of Bethany dressed as a slinky kitty for Halloween.

I might even have banged my head against the wall in despair. Just a little. But it was enough to cause an avalanche inside the closet. The next thing I knew, a huge pile of T-shirts had come tumbling down from the top shelf into my lap. The first shirt stuck its tongue out at me: *nyeh-nyeh boo-boo*.

I turned it over. Aha! The Rolling Stones.

The second T-shirt screamed for "HELP!"

The Beatles.

Okay, so some of these geezer bands on the T-shirts were familiar because my dad loves to humiliate me (and himself) by blasting classic rock in the car and playing air guitar at stoplights. Others I only sorta recognized, like the Velvet Underground, Pink Floyd, and Led Zeppelin, but it didn't really matter because the shirts were cool in an authentic and ancient kind of way. Best yet, they're not from the mall and were guaranteed NOT to be seen on anyone else at school! I could definitely wear something different every day and I wouldn't have to wear some crazy purple tuxedo jacket to do it! Woo-hoo!

With these shirts, I could totally cross off #1 on the IT List. As I gathered up the stack, I couldn't help but think that my big sister would be oh so proud of how ready I was to rock seventh grade.

Chapter Six

My first day of junior high! And what a day it was. Where to start?

I guess I should begin at the beginning with my parents' extra-special wake-up call. This basically consisted of Mom "dancing" around my bed while Dad played air guitar and sang a made-up song.

"Oh-oh-oh! Notso not-so-little no mo'. Oh-oh-oh!"

This had to be the most alarming morning alarm EVER. Bridget would have loved it. She would have sung and danced along. But I'm not Bridget. I shooed them away so they could channel their hyperness into more important efforts such as making me an extra-special first-day-of-school breakfast of blueberry pancakes and bacon.

Once they were out of the room, I slipped on my lucky

jeans and put on what I thought was the coolest of the old T-shirts that had fallen into my lap. It was for a band called the Who, but that didn't mean much to me. What I really liked about it was the red, white, and blue bull's-eye surrounding the band's logo. Pineville Junior High's colors are red, white, and blue so I thought that was a pretty clever way to show my school spirit without being a total brownnoser about it.

I washed my face, brushed my teeth, combed my hair, and pulled it back into a high ponytail. Mom won't let me wear anything bolder than tinted lip balm before I'm thirteen. I complain about how totally unfair this is but, in truth, it's fine by me because no make-upping means I'll do maybe five minutes of primping, max. I get to sleep in while girls like Bridget wake before sunrise to put their school faces on.

Speaking of, I was at the kitchen counter polishing off my third pancake when I heard the front door open. It was 7:20 a.m. on the dot—our appointed meeting time. I knew it was Bridget even before I heard my mom's squeal of delight.

"Bridget! What a lovely haircut!" Mom exclaimed.

I hastily wiped syrup off my chin with the back of my hand and met them in the foyer to investigate. It was true! Bridget had cut off her hair! It was much, much shorter now, about shoulder length. And white-blond bangs edged her blue eyes like the perfect picture frame. I'd hardly had time to react to the new hair when I noticed she wasn't wearing the outfit she'd settled on the day before. She'd traded the tee, capris, and slip-ons for a more sophisticated look: embroidered tank, swingy skirt, and strappy sandals. The overall effect was, like, *whoa*.

Mom was more articulate when she said, "It's like you grew up overnight!"

This compliment made Bridget smile from ear to ear, which revealed the most dramatic change of all: teeth! I was seeing Bridget's teeth for the first time in two and a half years!

"Bridget! You got your braces off!!! When???"

"Surprise!!! I know! Yesterday!!!"

Now that Bridget was smiling it was like she was physically incapable of *not* smiling. And I could hardly blame her. This makeover must have given her the confidence boost she needed because she wasn't at all red-faced and fidgety about our first day anymore. She had strapped on her backpack and was ready to take Pineville Junior High by storm!

"Photo op!"

Uh, right after Mom and Dad took about a bazillion pictures.

"Yay!" Bridget clapped and cheered. "Take lots of pictures for my mom, okay?"

This was a totally unnecessary request. Since the divorce three years ago, my parents had stepped in to document all of Bridget's most important moments because her mom was usually at work. In fact, Bridget's mom was already a few hours into her shift before we'd even made it to the bus stop. She was a waitress at Baygate Diner, a restaurant popular for its breakfast specials. Anyway, it wasn't too hard for my parents to capture the fourth-grade art show, fifth-grade band concert, or sixth-grade Moving On Up Ceremony, because Bridget's most important moments also happened to be *my* most important moments. The first day of seventh grade was just the latest, but it wouldn't be the last.

My parents didn't share any photos with Mr. Milhokovich. Bridget's dad has lived in California since the split. "He's little more to his daughter than a signature on child-support checks." That's what Bridget's mom says on Saturday nights after her double shift at the restaurant and a glass or two of pink wine.

Bridget spent most of the summer with her dad. She came back with tons of souvenirs from all the cool places she visited while she was on the West Coast—Universal Studios, Disneyland, the Academy Awards theater, and so on. She also came back with a blistery sunburn that just healed in time for school. She said the souvenirs were more painful than the sunburn, which I thought was strange until I witnessed Mrs. Milhokovich crying over the discovery of a Mickey Mouse plushie, a Hollywood sign key chain, and a Lakers T-shirt Bridget had stuffed deep into the kitchen trash can—but not deep enough.

It always made Bridget sad to talk about stuff like this, so we never talked about stuff like this, except when she decided she wanted to talk about stuff like this and she'd cry a lot and I'd feel guilty about complaining about how my dad acted like a dork when I was lucky to have a dad around at all. My parents really aren't that bad, I guess. They're just... you know. *Parents.* It's pretty much impossible to look at them like ordinary people when they're your own.

"Now say, 'Brie!'" Dad shouted.

"Brie!" Bridget shouted back.

I stood next to Bridget stiffly as she struck a pose like a runway pro.

"Now say, 'Gorgonzola!'"

"Gorgonzola!"

Bridget acted like smiling for pictures was the *funnest thing ever.* And the weird thing was, the more confidence Bridget projected as we posed and posed and posed for my parents, the less confident I felt about my own appearance—as if there was only so much awesomeness the universe could handle. What if there was a limited amount of confidence to go around? Like, if Bridget had self-assurance out the wazoo, there'd be less for the rest of the first-day-of-seventh-graders like me to share. As I strained to smile, I asked myself if I'd feel less loserish if I went upstairs and put on a safer outfit from the mall. Something more like Bridget's. And why didn't I get a stylish new haircut? Or braces? So what if I have naturally straight teeth? I could have gotten braces just to stun all of Pineville Junior High School with the dazzling sight of my naked teeth when I got them removed!

Bridget was still going along with my dad's cheesiness. Ha! In more ways than one.

"Monterey Jack!" Dad shouted.

"Monterey Jack!" Bridget shouted back.

I had just about convinced myself of the Limited Universal Confidence Theory when she stopped striking poses and turned her attention to me.

"I love your T-shirt! I wish I was cool enough to pull that off!"

And that's when Bridget reminded me why she's my *bestest friend ever.*

"You're cool enough, Bridget. Believe me."

Then I hooked my arm around hers and we set off for the bus stop.

Coolly. Confidently. Awesomely.

Together.

Chapter Seven

The bus ride to Pineville Junior High was like all other bus rides to school in that it was very, very loud. Selective hearing must be a mandatory trait for school bus drivers. For most of the ride Miz Carbone—the tattooed, toothpick-chewing lady behind the wheel—somehow managed to ignore the craziness going on behind her and concentrate on the road. Just when I thought she was totally zoned out—fantasizing about hitting the open road on her Harley instead of driving a bus full of screaming kids—she'd miraculously tune in to reprimand a rider for using profanity or otherwise inappropriate language.

"HEY NOW!" Miz Carbone yelled. "NO CUSSIN' WHEN I'M BUSSIN'."

I will bet a bazillion dollars she has this motto tattooed somewhere on her body.

Even though it was the first day of school, I was struck by how our school bus already had that very specific school bus smell, like scorched rubber, bag lunches gone bad, and…well…and a scent I can only describe as *armpit.*

The eighth graders had taken their rightful positions in the back of the bus while the rest of us were expected to fend for ourselves. Bridget and I silently slipped into an empty two-seater toward the rear-front, which was a pretty sweet spot for seventh graders. I knew I was as grateful for Bridget's company as she was for mine.

Apparently the eighth-grade boys were also appreciative of Bridget's presence on the bus. They went to very noisy lengths to let her know it.

"Yo, Bee Em Bee!"

"Hey, Bee Em Bee!"

"Yo, Bee Em Bee!"

Bridget ignored these *fascinating* attempts at conversation.

Boys my age are the most inarticulate creatures on the planet. They'll stick to single syllables unless it's a topic of conversation that's of major significance to their lives. As far as I can tell, their deepest discussions are limited to three subjects:

1. Sports
2. Video games
3. Farts

And my mother wonders why I haven't developed major crushes on any of my classmates. It's a nonissue anyway because apparently the feeling is mutual.

Back on the bus, the shouting continued.

"HEEEEEEY, BEEEE EMMMM BEEEE!"

"YOOOOOO, BEEEE EMMMM BEEEE!"

"I really hope we end up in at least one class together," Bridget was saying.

"Uh," I stammered. "What?"

It was almost impossible to concentrate on the conversation even though Bridget was seated right beside me.

"I was just making sure you picked Family and Consumer Sciences as your first choice for Exploratory."

"HEEEEEEY, BEEEEEEMMMMMMBEEEEEE!!!"

"YOOOOOO, BEEEEEEMMMMMMBEEEEEE!!!"

I couldn't take it anymore. She had to do something— wave or smile at them—whatever would shut them up. Or would that just rile them up even more?

"Bridget!" I hissed.

"What?"

"Them!" I jerked my thumb toward the boys in the back.

Then she looked up from her BMB-embroidered backpack, shrugged, and grinned at me without a trace of guile. Her smile was like the sun bursting through the clouds accompanied by a choir of angels. And that's when I realized that Bridget wasn't ignoring the boys because she was exhibiting the Miz Carbone–like superpower to NOT hear them. No, she ignored them because she had absolutely no clue that *she* was the person they were trying so hard to impress. It made me wonder if there'd ever been a time a group of boys had tried to win *my* approval—only to lose out to my own oblivious indifference. If I ever hope to make good on IT List #3: Pick your first boyfriend wisely, I better start paying closer attention. That's what I was thinking as the bus pulled us into the Pineville Junior High parking lot for the first time.

"We're here!" Bridget squealed with wide-eyed excitement.

The first homeroom warning bell was already ringing as we got off the bus. They didn't waste any time in junior high, did they? My homeroom and Bridget's were on opposite sides of the first floor, so we pretty much had to say goodbye as soon as we got inside. I really, really didn't want to find out what would happen if I showed up late, so I was all ready to take off when Bridget clutched both of my hands.

"If I don't see you again," she said as if she were going overseas, not just across the hall, "save me a seat on the bus ride home, okay?"

Before I could answer, one of the eighth graders from the back of the bus came over. He was the cute one, I guess, if I were forced to choose. Suntanned, tall, and broad-shouldered, he looked like he'd spent the entire summer outside throwing, catching, and running after things. This was undoubtedly true because he was wearing a PJHS Football T-shirt. His smile revealed a small space between his top front teeth, a flaw that somehow made him look even cuter than he already was, you know, if you're into the jock type. Which I'm not. I don't think I have a "type" yet. How am I supposed to pick my first boyfriend wisely if I don't have a type?

"I'm Burke Roy," the cute jock said to Bridget. "I'll save you a seat on the ride home."

Burke Roy clearly didn't require orthodontic perfection to boost *his* mojo. Bridget just about melted under the warmth of his gap-toothed grin. He took this as a sign of encouragement and stepped right between us.

"I'll be your one-man welcome committee," he continued, taking her by the elbow.

As the final warning bell rang, I watched Burke escort Bridget to her classroom. She didn't even turn to say good-bye or good luck. This boy she'd known for less than twelve seconds had made her forget all about the best friend she'd known for more than twelve years. I hadn't even gotten to homeroom yet and I'd already discovered five hard truths about junior high:

1. My best friend had turned pretty.
2. She didn't know it yet.
3. It wouldn't be long before she did.
4. That knowledge would change everything between us.
5. And there wasn't a thing I could do about it.

Chapter Eight

Today was the first time kids from our town's four elementary schools merged into one harmonious seventh-grade class of two hundred students. My school was the smallest of the four so I was one of only twenty Pineville Elementary students who moved up to the junior high. I had way fewer friends and familiar faces than the lucky graduates from Beach Pines Elementary, who were one hundred strong.

I tried not to be discouraged by this social disadvantage.

Homerooms were arranged alphabetically by last name. Room 102 included the second half of the Cs, all the Ds and Es, and the beginning of the Fs. IT List #4, Stick with the IT clique, weighed heavily on my mind, so I was a bit stressed about finding the "right" person to sit with. Would I even recognize the "right" person when I saw her?

(Or *him*, I guess. I have to get used to being more open-minded about boys.) I was actually kind of relieved when I didn't get to decide for myself. My name was on a placard designating my assigned seat: two rows from the left, second seat from the front.

I had to pass by the first girl in the row to get to my seat. She had dark curly hair and was wearing an outfit very similar to the one Bridget had picked out for herself that morning—only she's shorter and stockier than Bridget so it looked different on her. Not bad, just different. I couldn't help but notice that she was watching me very carefully as I squeezed past the pricy designer backpack that she had thrown carelessly in the aisle between the rows, like she was afraid I'd step on the rhinestone strap or something.

I had barely sat down when this girl spun around in her seat and introduced herself.

"I'm Sara," she said. "*D'Abruzzi.*"

She put special emphasis on her last name, which for some reason made me feel like I should do the same.

"I'm Jessica," I replied. "*Darling.*"

I probably should've stopped there, but I didn't.

"I guess it's our alphabetical destiny to be seated together."

Sara squinted her eyes, giving me a curious look. Sometimes I say too much. This might have been one of those times.

"Omigod! Yeah! I guess you're right!" she said, laughing.

I released a sigh of relief.

"So you probably recognize my name. D'Abruzzi."

I didn't.

"Because my dad is Wally D'Abruzzi."

This still meant nothing to me.

"My family practically owns the entire Boardwalk," she said, ticking off his business ventures on her hand. "There's Wally D's Sweet Treat Shoppe, Winning Wally's Arcade…"

Oh! I knew those places! I love the candy apples at the sweet shop and kick major Skee-Ball butt at the arcade! I was going to tell her this, but I never got the chance because Sara D'Abruzzi just kept right on talking. And talking. And talking.

Sara said she has two stepbrothers who are much younger than she is and total snot-nosed monsters and she also has an older brother named Joe who's a senior varsity football player at Pineville High and totally cool and her two BFFs from Beach Pines Elementary have crushes on him even though they've totally denied it, especially someone named Hope because she's always like, "Oh, Joe totally isn't my type," and then Sara's like, "Omigod! Cool football players aren't your type?" and then someone named Manda's like, "Cool football players are my type!"

and then the Hope person is all, "Every guy is your type!" which Sara said is totally, totally true. And when she took a breath I was able to ask, "Who are these girls you're talking about?" and Sara was like, "Omigod! You'll totally meet them and totally love them!" and I was feeling a bit woozy and overwhelmed by this information overload and was super-relieved when our homeroom teacher passed out our schedules and Sara *finally* stopped talking.

For about a second.

"Gimme!" Sara said, grabbing my schedule out of my hands before I'd looked at it myself. "Omigod! Our schedules are practically twinsies!"

It turned out that Sara D'Abruzzi was also in the Gifted & Talented classes. What luck to have met a new G&T friend in my very first minutes of seventh grade! In fact, all our classes were the same. Except eighth period.

"Ew," Sara said, curling her lip. "What's up with your Exploratory?"

I had no idea what was up with my Exploratory because I hadn't had a chance to review it myself. Sara handed it over to me, looking grim.

"Industrial Arts?" I questioned aloud. "What the heck is that?"

"Omigod! I think it's"—Sara paused dramatically— "Woodshop!"

Then she quickly covered her mouth with her hand, as if she'd just said *Witchcraft* instead of *Woodshop*.

"I asked for Family and Consumer Sciences," I complained. "Not this!"

To be honest, I wasn't really thrilled with the idea of taking Family and Consumer Sciences either, which is just a fancy way of saying Home Ec. I only checked off that box because Bridget begged me to. It was probably our only chance at having a class together. Otherwise, I would've picked Creative Writing.

"You need to get that switched," Sara said, all serious. "Like, pronto."

I spent the rest of homeroom fretting about how I would go about righting this wrong. Then the bell rang and we got up to go to our lockers for the first time, which is when I found out that lockers are also arranged alphabetically by last name, guaranteeing that Darling, Jessica would be seeing a lot of D'Abruzzi, Sara.

So Sara and I headed off for the first of our seven periods together: Language Arts with Miss Orden. Miss Orden was a wispy willow in a billowy gypsy skirt. She would lift off like a balloon in even the slightest breeze if she weren't anchored to the earth by her chunky vegan footwear. Her voice quivered with passion for literature like a string on Cupid's bow.

"S. E. Hinton was fifteen—hardly older than all of you—when she—yes, *she*—began writing *The Outsiders.*"

Miss Orden looked hardly any older than some of the more, uh, *developed* girls in our class. Her face was without makeup or care, as if she'd never had a worry in all of her cruelty-free life. Bethany would happily kidnap her for an ambush makeover.

"What do you think of that?" she asked the class.

There were about twenty-five of us, none of whom had come from my elementary school or looked the least bit interested in answering her question. I really hate awkward silences. The only thing I hate even more than awkward silences is my unstoppable urge to fill them.

"S. E. Hinton was so young when she wrote it," I offered. "She was still in touch with how it feels to be an outsider."

Miss Orden nodded, her earrings all ajangle, encouraging me to go on.

"That's why readers are able to relate to the story even though it's from a totally different time period."

Miss Orden responded with a fist pump and a resounding "YES!" followed by, "What does the rest of the class think?"

And the rest of the class responded with shuffled feet, averted eyes, and wordless murmurs. It didn't seem possible—or fair—that all these students had scored higher than Bridget on the G&T entrance exam.

That's when it hit me: I was the only one in the room who had actually done the mandatory summer reading! Or maybe it was even worse than that. Maybe everyone else had done the mandatory reading but had gotten the memo that it was totally uncool to acknowledge that they had done the mandatory reading by raising their hands and offering an insightful opinion about the mandatory reading that they were only pretending not to have read.

WHY WASN'T INSIDE INFORMATION LIKE THAT ON MY SISTER'S IT LIST?

And just when I was convinced that I'd doomed the Darling name to dorkdom on the very first day of my very first class in junior high, I was saved by Sara's friend from elementary school. The one named—appropriately enough—Hope.

"She used her youth to her advantage," Hope began. "Adults have no clue what it's like to be young. It's like they totally forget everything they went through when they were growing up. S. E. Hinton didn't have to remember. She was living it."

There were two things about Hope that you couldn't help but notice right away: her height and her hair. She was definitely the tallest girl in G&T, maybe even the whole school. She might even have been taller than the tallest boy. And if that weren't attention-getting enough, her height was topped off with a mass of the brightest orangy-red hair only ever seen on characters animated by Disney.

Unlike many tall girls with unignorable hair, Hope didn't try to hide. She had spoken with confidence. The result? Miss Orden looked like she had died and gone to Language Arts heaven.

When that class ended and we went to second period, Sara officially introduced me to Hope and also to Manda, who happened to be one of the, uh, *developed* girls I mentioned earlier. The four of us went to Spanish together taught by Señora Epstein (NOT pronounced *ep-STINE* or *ep-STEEN* but *ape-stay-EE-en*, which I guess is supposed to sound more Spanishlike). The four of us pretty much stuck together all day, through Pre-Algebra, Physical Science with Mr. Todd (better known as Mr. Odd because there's a definite spaciness about him, like he's inhaled the chemical contents of too many test tubes), Social Studies, and Gym, but I'm not really going to get into all that right now because everything that led up to my seventh and eighth periods is kind of blurry.

Lunch and Woodshop were *doozies*.

Chapter Nine

Lunch was seventh period. However, preparations for lunch began much earlier in the day. Lunch was pretty much the only period we could decide who we wanted to sit with and where. According to Sara, the importance of these decisions could not be underestimated. So much so that she'd persuaded Hope—the artistic one, apparently—to draw up a map of the cafeteria based on what Sara had learned during her extensive research on the subject.

"The round tables in the center of the room are our best bet," she said during a lull in Language Arts.

"Best bet for what?" I asked.

"Staking our claim."

Next period, in Spanish class, Sara picked up right where she had left off.

"We can watch the Hots at the long tables without getting in their way."

"The Hots?" I asked.

"The popular crowd," Sara explained. "And we won't get mistaken for the Nots at the square tables near the kitchen."

"The Nots?" I asked. "The unpopular kids?"

Sara closed her eyes and nodded serenely, like I was the rookie ninja and I had just bested my master.

Finally, in Social Studies, Sara further explained why the round tables were ideal for our group. Sara really likes explaining things.

"There's room for four to six people, which is the perfect number because it's exclusive without being snobby."

At which point our Social Studies teacher, Miss Hutch, confiscated the cafeteria map and joked, "That's not the kind of geography we'll be focusing on here."

The class laughed, but Sara did not. This was serious business.

She expressed her annoyance on the way to the cafeteria.

"Omigod! Choosing the perfect lunch table is probably the most important Social Studying I'll do all year," she said in a huff. "You'll thank me for doing my research."

And when we stepped through the double doors and

experienced the cafeteria firsthand, I knew she was right. The cafeteria was like the riot of the school bus multiplied by, like, a bazillion. The everything-goes state of the lunchroom was even more shocking because of the strict assigned-seat structure that had come all morning. We were frozen in place, not knowing where we'd fit in amid the chaos.

Fortunately, Sara knew just where to go. She was our fearless leader and took on the role with gusto.

"OMIGOD! RIGHT THERE!" she yelled, pointing to an empty round table. "THAT'S OUR SPOT!"

Two mousy girls were timidly drifting in the general direction of the same table. I knew one of them from elementary school: Dori Sipowitz. She was plain and soft spoken, and I knew that Sara would consider her a classic Not.

"QUICK! BEFORE THEY STEAL IT!" Hope squealed.

Sara and Hope rushed for that round table as if it were the last lifeboat on the *Titanic*. Manda and I quickly followed. We all slapped down our backpacks and victoriously claimed the table as our own.

"Woo-hoo!" Manda cheered. "High fives all around!"

Sara held up her hand first. I followed. Then Hope. Only when all hands were in the air did Manda officially offer us her congratulations. It was strange how Manda led the celebration of the round table even though Sara and Hope had done all the work to get it. But I didn't think about it all that much because I was too busy feeling guilty as I watched Dori and her sorry-looking friend slink away. Having accepted their fate, they steered themselves toward the square tables near the kitchen.

I guess this is where I should mention that Dori Sipowitz and I used to be friends.

Okay. *Best* friends.

When we were in single digits, Dori, Bridget, and I were an inseparable trio. I was the one who came up with the name 3ZNUF, which we all thought was incredibly clever in elementary school. Our motto?

"3ZNUF! 4EVA!"

On the weekends, 3ZNUF would gather at Dori's house because Bridget's mom was always mad at her dad and my mom always complained too much about the noise and the mess. We'd play make-believe games like School (I was the teacher, they were the students), Bank (I was the teller, they were the customers), or Store (I was the cashier, they were the shoppers). I can't even fathom how many peanut butter and jelly sandwiches I must have eaten in Dori's daisy-yellow kitchen. Bridget's mom was usually too preoccupied to make lunch for us. And my mom tried too hard to fancy up our PB&J by buying plum preserves or lingonberry jam. When I was little, all I wanted was plain old grape jelly.

And I guess that sort of became the problem with Dori.

She was the friendship equivalent of plain old grape jelly. Dori was by far the most reliable of the three of us. She never forgot to give me the red Skittles and Bridget the yellow ones. She never hoarded the sharpest colored pencils. She never borrowed an American Girl doll and forgot to return it. We could always count on Dependable Dori.

As single digits turned into double digits, Bridget became obsessed with Hollywood gossip and the hottest fashions. I really got into books, especially my sister's old paperbacks, dozens of novels about gorgeous sixteen-year-old twins who—based on the cover art, anyway—must have reminded Bethany of herself. Dori just kept being Dori. She was content to keep playing School and Bank and Store. But Bridget and I...well...we just weren't anymore.

Dependable Dori turned into Predictable Dori. Predictable Dori turned into Boring Dori. And, yes, I was the one who started calling her Doring behind her back, but Bridget didn't exactly resist. I'm also not proud to admit that I was incredibly relieved when Dori's family moved into a bigger house across town during the summer before fifth grade. Across town might as well have been across the galaxy. By the time Bridget and I graduated from sixth grade, 3ZNUF was a faded memory.

Faded, not forgotten. Definitely not 4EVA. There was still enough of *something* there between us to try to save her from sitting at a Not table.

"Uh, maybe we could invite them to sit with us," I suggested. "There's room...."

Hope raised an eyebrow. Sara blinked in disbelief. Manda batted her eyelashes and locked her arm in mine.

"Jess! You are the sweetest girl *ever* for taking pity on those two poor Nots," she said in a sugary tone. "Isn't she?" She didn't bother looking to Sara and Hope for verification. "You really live up to your last name!"

Then she headed toward the lunch line without discussing the matter any further. We would not be inviting Dori and her friend to sit with us. That was that.

As we followed after Manda, Sara took it upon herself to explain the Unbreakable Laws of Cafeteria Line Cutting.

"The *what*?" I asked, unsure I had heard her correctly.

"The Unbreakable Laws of Cafeteria Line Cutting," Sara said. "Obey or die."

This system had been passed down orally from student to student through the generations. In that way it was kind of like the epic battle songs by the ancient Greek poets—only with even greater threat of bloodshed if the laws were broken.

The Unbreakable Laws of Cafeteria Line Cutting

1. **8th-Grade Hots** can cut everyone, anytime, anywhere. The hottest 8th-Grade Hots (Hot Plusses) often bypass the line altogether by

making 8th-Grade Hot Minuses purchase their lunches for them while they hold court at the long tables by the windows. Particularly promising 7th-Grade Hots can be tapped for lunch-buying duty, which is considered a great honor. It's kind of like an apprenticeship for popularity.

2. **8th-Grade Hot Minuses** can cut everyone except the 8th-Grade Hots who actually buy their own lunches.

3. **8th-Grade Normals** can cut any seventh grader. They can be granted temporary Hot Minus line-cutting privileges if they are wearing something really, really cute or have just scored the winning point in a big game. (This often indicates that the Normal is on the verge of a promotion to Hot Minus status.)

4. **7th-Grade Hots** can cut all seventh graders and all Nots.

5. **7th-Grade Hot Minuses** can cut 7th-Grade Normals and all Nots.

6. **7th-Grade Normals** can cut all Nots.

7. **8th-Grade Nots** can cut 7th-Grade Nots.

8. **7th-Grade Nots** can't cut anyone. Ever. If they don't brown bag it, they don't eat at all.

Why wasn't *this* on my sister's IT List? This was practical information I could use, if only to avoid getting trampled by a ravenous eighth grader who wouldn't let anything—or anyone—get between him and his sloppy joe sandwich.

"What are we?" I asked as an eighth-grade boy with, like, a full-grown mustache went straight to the front without any objection.

"It's only the first day so we all start out as 7th-Grade Normals." She paused long enough to make eye contact with Dori Sipowitz and her hapless friend who had gotten in line before us. "Unless you're obviously a Not."

I watched with discomfort as Sara boldly pushed ahead of the two girls. Manda didn't think twice about staking the spot in front of Sara.

"Such a sweetie!" Manda said to no one in particular. "Such a doll!"

Manda's words were kind, but her tone was not. And I had no idea who she was addressing. Sara? Me? Dori and all the "sweeties" and "dolls" she was cutting on line? Like those bogus terms of endearment were supposed to make us feel better about what she was doing? I awkwardly stood in front of the trash can, wringing my hands and wondering what to do. I was thinking that Hope had the right idea by bringing her own lunch.

"Jessica!" Sara snapped. "Come on! What are you waiting for?"

I was waiting to grow a backbone. To stand tall and strong enough to say, *Hey, I know that everyone cuts everyone and that's the way it's been forever and nobody questions it, but I don't think it's fair and even though Dori and I aren't friends anymore we do have a history together and I'd feel like a total jerk if I cut her—*

Dori nudged me, interrupting my inner monologue.

"Go ahead," she mouthed. She didn't look at me though. She kept her eyes on the dimes in her penny loafers.

Dori Sipowitz has been wearing dimes in her penny loafers since preschool.

Grape jelly.

Sigh.

Grape jelly.

Dori had barely stepped aside when Sara grabbed the hem of my shirt and pulled me toward her and Manda.

"This is where we belong," Sara assured me.

"For now," Manda said. "We'll be 7th-Grade Hots before we know it!"

I honestly didn't know how I felt about that. I still don't.

Even with my slight social edge, there were only about five minutes left in the lunch period by the time I got my French fries and grilled cheese sandwich. I had just sat down when Sara called our attention to something going on behind me.

"Omigod! Who is *that*?"

"Whoever she is, she's getting a personal escort from the boys' football team," Hope observed.

"Whoever she is, she's on the fast track to Hot!" Sara exclaimed.

Manda put on her glasses to get a better look. She wrinkled her nose at whatever she saw.

I turned around to see for myself. A bunch of boys wearing identical PJHS Football T-shirts had joined Burke Roy on what was now Bridget's Seven-Man Welcome Committee. After the scene on the bus this morning, I shouldn't have been surprised to see that all this fuss was being made over someone whose most distinguishing characteristics—until yesterday—were a braid down to her butt, a mouth full of metal, and hives. Wow. What a difference a day makes.

Bridget spotted me right away. A look of relief washed over her face.

"JESSICA!" Bridget shouted loud enough for the whole cafeteria to hear.

She ran toward our table without so much as a glance in the football team's direction.

"You know her?" Sara asked incredulously. "Who is she?"

"That's Bridget," I said. "My best friend from Pineville Elementary."

"You didn't mention that your best friend is totally gorgeous," Sara said.

"She's not *totally* gorgeous," Manda replied dismissively. "She's, like, sorta gorgeous."

"That makes no sense," Hope piped in. "By the definition of gorgeousness, nothing can be just 'sorta' gorgeous...."

"Then she's not gorgeous," Manda sniffed just as Bridget breathlessly reached the table.

By her own definition, Manda is also not gorgeous. Pretty but not gorgeous. And it's a kind of pretty that required effort. Like, there's no way she woke up with hair so pin-straight and shiny. And she must have done a lot of research before she found the exact color of eyeliner to make her gray eyes pop. And she was obviously aware of how to make the most of her, um, most notable assets. Let's put it this way: If what I wore was considered a training bra, Manda's was a two-time world champion.

Bridget crashed down beside me and crushed me in a hug.

"I feel like I haven't seen you since forever! I kept hoping you'd show up in one of my classes, and I'm so relieved we have lunch together. I'm starving!"

She opened up her lunch bag, tore off the plastic wrap on her turkey sandwich, and unselfconsciously started eating. Bridget was oblivious to the reaction she was getting from all the boys…and the girls at my table…and everyone.

"I got totally lost on the way to the cafeteria," she began in between chews, "and then those nice guys on the football team offered to help me find my way, but they have a worse sense of direction than I do because somehow we ended up on the totally wrong floor on the totally wrong side of the building and…"

As Bridget babbled on, Sara's eyes got wider and wider and wider while Manda's eyes got narrower and narrower and narrower. Hope's expression was unreadable. In fact, I'm not sure she was even listening.

Bridget took the final bite of her sandwich and washed it down with gulps of iced tea. She had just started in on her bag of pretzels when she paused and looked across the table.

"Sheesh! You must think I'm, like, the rudest girl ever!" She brushed pretzel salt off her hands. "I'm Jess's best friend. I'm Bridget!"

"Jessica has told us all about you," Hope replied with a slight smile.

"No, she hasn't," Manda replied without a smile.

"There's always more to know about everyone," Sara replied with the biggest smile of all. "Like, where did you get that adorable skirt? I love it!"

Bridget lit up. "I was just about to ask you where *you* got *your* adorable skirt!"

Sara's and Bridget's adorable skirts were exactly the same. So Sara told Bridget where she bought her adorable skirt and then Bridget told Sara where she bought her adorable skirt and—WOULDN'T YOU KNOW IT?—it turned out that they had bought their same exact adorable skirts at the same exact store. In fact, the other three girls were all wearing clothes that not only looked like they came from the same exact store, but from the same exact rack. More than ever was I baffled by what my sister was thinking with "Wear something different every day."

I swear Manda read my mind.

"Jessica, I've been meaning to ask you all day. Where did you get your shirt?"

"It's vintage!" I said proudly, having prepared the answer in advance.

"It's . . ." Manda puckered her lips. "Um." More puckering. "Interesting."

Interesting.

Interesting is . . . good? Right? Interesting is the opposite of boring. It means I'm not grape jelly. I'm lingonberry jam!

Right?

Sigh. I really don't understand fashion.

Talk turned to the last period of the day, and Bridget was thrilled to discover that she and her adorable skirt would be joining Sara, Manda, and Hope for Home Ec. She was not thrilled when she found out that I wouldn't be joining them but not as unthrilled as I was about this situation.

"Woodshop?" Bridget recoiled. "What happened to Family and Consumer Sciences?"

"I don't know what happened," I replied. "I specifically requested *not Woodshop*."

"You really need to get that switched," Sara said, echoing the warning from homeroom. "Pronto."

"Don't expect much from your guidance counselor," Hope said.

It was the first comment she had directed at me all day.

"Uh, okay," I replied, unsure of whether I even had a guidance counselor, let alone where that person might be located in the building.

"They *hate* changing around schedules," Hope added. "Which is *lame* because it's their *job*." She sounded surprisingly bitter about this, like she was speaking from experience.

Then the bell rang and the whole room sprang up from their respective tables to make the mad dash to last period. Only Hope held back a bit.

"Have you *seen* Mr. Poodle?" Hope asked.

"Mr. Poodle?" I said, giggling at the name. "Who's that?"

"The Woodshop teacher," Hope said. "My brother warned me about him. He said I should avoid the Woodshop hallway at all costs."

I rolled my eyes.

"You're avoiding someone named after a yippy fur ball?"

Hope gave me a pointed look. "That's exactly what I'm saying."

And then she jogged to catch up with the rest of the girls on their way to Home Ec. I honestly don't know what to make of Hope. Though I appreciate how she rescued me in Language Arts, she's otherwise kind of a bummer. She definitely hasn't gone out of her way to get to know me like Sara and Manda. Hmm. Maybe I'm not artsy enough for her.

Another thing I'll say about Hope is this: She was totally right to warn me about Woodshop.

Chapter Ten

Eighth period. Woodshop. THE CLASS I'M NOT SUP-POSED TO BE IN.

It's not a coincidence that the Woodshop classroom was in the farthest, darkest corner of the school. No one would just accidentally wander back there. Obviously school administrators didn't want unsuspecting seventh graders getting lost (cue spooky music and evil laughter) ONLY NEVER TO RETURN. Nope, the only one who had to fear for her life was the innocent seventh-grade girl who was assigned Woodshop even though she specifically requested NOT WOODSHOP.

There was a beautiful wooden sign hanging on the door, its border intricately carved in folk-artsy vines. It read:

MR. PUDEL'S WOODSHOP
(FOLLOW MY RULES AND NOBODY DIES)

This did not make me feel any better about my personal safety.

I had barely recovered from this warning when the man himself emerged from the back of the workshop. *Man* is an understatement. Mr. Pudel is a...a...

"Monster!" he roared. "Sasquatch! Bigfoot!"

I was thinking *Giant*, but those other options would suffice.

"Now that I've gotten that out of the way, allow me to officially introduce myself. My name"—he paused dramatically—"is Mr. Pudel."

When Hope said it, I shook with laughter. When Mr. Pudel said it, I shook with fear. Not everyone was intimidated, however. This was a class full of tough kids. One of them started yipping like a teeny dog because this is how tough kids show how tough they are: with feats of stupidity. Why else would he mock a giant who could squish him like a grape underfoot?

"P-U-D-E-L," Mr. Pudel spelled, pointing to the sign on the door. "Not P-O-O-D-L-E."

More boys joined in on the yipping. Mr. Pudel ignored them.

"This is Woodshop. Not Industrial Arts or whatever fancy name the board of education wants to give it. Woodshop." He paused and looked around the room. "Welcome to Woodshop."

I also took this opportunity to look around the workshop. It was at that moment I realized that not only was I the only non-tough kid in the class, but I was the only girl! How did this happen?

I timidly raised my hand.

"Uh, excuse me, uh...Mr...."

"P-U-D-E-L," our teacher repeated calmly. "It's Ukrainian."

"Mr. Pudel...uh...sir."

Mr. Pudel bearing down on me was bad enough. But all the tough kids had turned around on their stools and were staring at me, too. I couldn't help but notice that they weren't looking at me in the googly-eyed way the bus boys and the football team had looked at Bridget. They were looking at me like, "What the heck is she doing here?"

I couldn't agree more.

"Uh," I stammered. "I don't think I'm supposed to be in this class."

That's when Mr. Pudel broke out into song.

"Whoooooo are you?" he sang. *"Doot doot. Doot doot."*

It was only slightly less mortifying than when my dad

sings, simply because I'm not related to my crazy Wood-shop teacher.

"Uh, I'm. Uh...I mean, my name is..."

"Your shirt," he said, gesturing with a beardy chin thrust. "The Who."

I looked down, having totally forgotten all about my T-shirt.

"*Whooooo are you?*" he repeated. "*Doot doot. Doot doot.*"

I smiled weakly and willed myself not to faint.

"Jessica Darling," I blurted.

Mr. Pudel reached behind himself and picked up the first piece of paper he laid his hand on. He "hmm-hmmed" over it for a second, then spoke.

"You're on the class roster," he said. "You're supposed to be here."

The "class roster" was definitely *not* a class roster. It was a delivery menu for Pineville Pizza Company. I certainly wasn't going to be the one who pointed this out.

Fortunately, I didn't have to. Because at that moment a latecomer walked through the door, a skinny redhead who looked as though he'd used a rabid squirrel for a hairbrush that morning. He muttered something as a greeting. I couldn't make it out, but whatever it was did not escape the superior function of Mr. Pudel's gigantic ears.

"What's that?" Mr. Pudel asked, casting a shadow over the late kid.

"I said," replied the late kid, " 'What's up, Hagrid?' "

The room fell silent. Then Mr. Pudel broadsided us all with booming laughter.

"HAHAHAHAHAHA. I've been teaching here for fifteen years. I thought I'd heard them all. Hagrid! From Harry Potter! That's a good one! HAHAHAHAHAHA."

Mr. Pudel said it in a way that was sort of complimentary but also made it clear that he wouldn't laugh so hard if he heard it again.

"I won't answer to Hagrid or Paul Bunyan or Balrog or BFG or Jolly Green or Godzilla or any of those other names you'll be tempted to call me behind my back. You will, however, answer to whatever name I call you. You see, I've got this rare brain disorder that makes it difficult for me to recognize faces and remember names...."

A tough kid with a crew cut blew a farty raspberry.

"That's bull—"

"Oh, is it, Mr. Mouth? I've got a doctor's note to prove it!"

Then Mr. Pudel tossed aside the delivery menu, opened his desk drawer, and pulled out what was obviously a half-finished crossword puzzle torn out of a newspaper.

"See? Proof! From a medical doctor!" He waved the

paper around in the air before shoving it back in the drawer with a satisfied "Ha!"

At this point there was no doubt that there was something unusual going on in Mr. Pudel's brain, and remembering our names was the least of it.

"So if I point at Aleck," he said, gesturing at the crazy-haired latecomer, "and yell, 'Hey, Aleck! Watch what you're doing with that circular saw!' Aleck here better watch out instead of whining that his name isn't Aleck."

"That's not fair," complained the boy now known as Aleck. "We deserve the same—"

"LIFE ISN'T FAIR!" Mr. Pudel roared, holding his right hand up for all of us to see. "I'm missing three fingers! You think that's fair?"

Holy cow! No ring, middle, or index fingers! Instead of a wave, Mr. Pudel's hand was caught in a permanent hang ten gesture. All of us—including Aleck and the rest of the tough kids—yelped something along the lines of "Holy cow!" and scrambled backward off our stools.

Mr. Pudel laughed heartily. Then his middle and ring fingers magically popped in place where they should be. We all screamed and fell off our stools again.

"Gotcha!" he bellowed. "I'm only missing ONE finger!"

The thing is, I know Mr. Pudel has probably pulled this prank at least a bazillion times in his life and he still thinks it's as hilarious as the first time he thought of it.

We were all grateful when the bell rang. We had made it through Woodshop with our lives—and our fingers—intact. I was more determined than ever to meet with my guidance counselor—whoever and wherever that person was—and get me the heck out of this class where I so clearly did not belong!

I had almost made it out the door when a huge weight clamped on my shoulder and spun me around. I think Mr. Pudel was smiling at me, but it was hard to see any of his teeth through his beard.

"Gifted and Talented, right?" he asked.

I nodded meekly.

"Did you know that Woodshop connects real life with the classroom?" he asked.

I shook my head.

"It encourages problem solving and reinforces lessons learned in math, science, and social studies."

I nodded again.

"I look forward to having you in my class," Mr. Pudel said with a definitive tone that would override any guidance counselor.

Minutes later I ran into Sara at our lockers. She smelled like butter and brown sugar. While I was fighting for my life in Woodshop, my friends were in Home Ec baking chocolate chip cookies.

To quote Mr. Pudel: LIFE ISN'T FAIR.

71

Bridget got to the bus before I did. She was politely explaining to a boy in a backward baseball cap—a boy who was a shorter, scrawnier, not-as-cute version of Burke Roy—that, no, he couldn't sit next to her because she was saving the seat for her best friend and, no, he couldn't have a chocolate chip cookie because she had also saved it for her best friend.

"Woo-hoo!" she called out. "There's my best friend now!"

And in that moment, after everything that had happened on my first day of seventh grade, I was so grateful that best friend was still me.

Chapter Eleven

My sister showed up at the house that night while Dad was out on his bike and Mom was at an open house. I think Bethany was anxious to hear about my first day of junior high.

I was less anxious to tell her about it.

Okay, despite my near-death experience in eighth period, I guess it was pretty successful as far as first days of seventh grade go. Yet I'd kind of hoped Bethany would be too busy tonight to find out how it went. I didn't have the heart to tell her that I had failed miserably at #1 on the IT List. I mean, can my vintage shirt be considered trendy when the only person who appreciated it was my crazy Woodshop teacher?

I assumed, at least, Bethany would be happy to see me wearing it.

I was wrong.

I ran in for a hug, but she held her arms out to stop me like I was contagious.

"What on earth are you wearing?!" she cried out.

"I found your T-shirts!" I said. "I wore this one for the first day!"

"T-shirts?" Bethany spluttered.

"All those cool ol—I mean *vintage*—T-shirts at the top of your closet...."

The next noise I heard was barely human.

"Noooooooooooooo! You weren't supposed to find those gross T-shirts in my closet! You were supposed to find the Style Inventories!"

"The what?"

Then she grabbed me by the hand and dragged me into her bedroom, the whole time going on about how Mom was supposed to have donated that trash bag of T-shirts to Goodwill a long time ago. She pointed sternly at the closet door.

"Go to the back of my closet right now," she directed. "Next to the shoe tree is a shelf with a stack of notebooks. The Style Inventories!"

I did as I was told and found a library of spiral notebooks in bright colors. PRIVATE PROPERTY OF BETHANY DARLING was written on every one.

"Heeeeey," I said. "I thought you said you didn't keep a diary because popular girls don't keep diaries...."

"Those are not diaries! They are Style Inventories! They document what I wore to school between the seventh and twelfth grades!"

She took the yellow one labeled SEVENTH GRADE, flipped it open to the first page, and handed it to me for my inspection. Every line was filled with my sister's bubbly handwriting:

9/4 Pink top, denim skirt, espadrilles, flowered headband
9/5 Blue cami, capris, sporty flats, butterfly clip
9/6 Striped mini dress, silver sandals, star barrette

I skipped ahead a few pages.

10/22 Fuzzy cardigan, pink top, plaid mini, black boots

And a few more.

11/6 Ribbed turtleneck, denim skirt, sporty flats

"I wanted you to consult these for inspiration!" my sister was shouting. "To show you how—with clever mix-and-matching and accessorizing and borrowing from friends—it was possible to never repeat the same outfit."

And that's when I realized the intended definition of IT List #1: Wear something different every day.

"Different" meaning dissimilar. Not "different" meaning unusual.

Bridget had the right idea all along with endless combinations of outfits, but I was too clueless to realize it!

My sister took calming breaths from a lotus position on the floor.

"All is not lost. There's hope for you yet. Tryouts are next week, correct? We'll just put this disaster behind us and move on to number two."

IT List #2: Make the CHEER TEAM!!!

Ack. I'd been dreading shouty #2 with all its exclamation points. In fact, I'd kind of hoped that I rocked #1 so hard that I could just skip over #2 and maybe the rest of the IT List entirely. My sister had other ideas.

"Let's see your best cheer."

My best cheer? I didn't have *a* cheer, let alone a best one.

"Uh?" I said. "Go team, go?"

Spirit fingers. Clap.

That was all I had.

My sister pressed her face into her hands and moaned.

"I see that I'm going to have to call in a favor."

In an instant, Bethany had sprung up from the floor and was on the phone. Most of the half conversation I heard didn't make much sense to me. From what I could figure out, she was talking to someone named Sherri about this year's CHEER TEAM!!! She said some things about awesomeness and asked a few questions about an arrow and said some more things about awesomeness and asked a few more questions about a gap and then she laughed a fake laugh and said good-bye and turned on me with fierce intensity.

"Bring me a tape measure!" she commanded.

"But...what?"

"Bring me a tape measure!"

It was clear she wasn't going to answer any of my questions until I brought her a tape measure.

I don't know about your house, but the Darling family doesn't have, like, a designated space set aside for tape measures. I thought it might be in Dad's tool kit but it wasn't and then I thought it might be in Mom's sewing basket but it wasn't and finally I had the good sense to look in our junk drawer, where it was caught in a brutal melee with a broken can opener, a length of twine, and about a bazillion packets of soy sauce. I disentangled the mess and returned to Bethany's room.

"Tape measure," I said.

"Stand up straight," she ordered.

Bethany extended the tape measure from my head to my feet.

"Hmmm..." she grumbled discouragingly. "Okay, maybe not *that* straight."

"Are you going to tell me what this is all ab—?"

"Shhh! Slouch! But just a little!"

I tried my best to do as instructed.

"No! That's too much! Just, like, a squinch."

I didn't know what a *squinch* was, but I must have figured it out because when I shrunk down just the teeniest bit, Bethany squealed and clapped in approval.

"Sixty-four inches! That's it! You're perfect!"

Now you have to understand something here. My popular, pretty big sister—she who had been officially voted Miss Perfect by her Pineville Junior High graduating class—was calling *me* perfect.

We were having a *moment.* I can honestly say that we had never shared a *moment* before. Not like this.

And I still had no idea what she was talking about.

"Let's see," my sister was saying. "Your hair is just long enough for the regulation ponytail. Obviously, you'll have to pad your bra. But otherwise, you're perfect."

There was that word again.

"Can you please tell me what's going on?"

Then my sister explained that the Sherri she called earlier was her co-captain on the CHEER TEAM!!! Sherri, or Miss Garcia, is now the Pineville Junior High School CHEER TEAM!!! coach. My sister asked her for TOP SECRET INFORMATION.

"She revealed that there is a very specific gap in The Alignment!" my sister enthused. "A gap that you are going to fill!"

None of this information helped me know any more than I did before she opened her mouth. My sister, patience waning, explained that an eighth grader named Annalise Shapiro had been injured in a tragic leg-waxing accident. Until the scabs stopped oozing, there was a gap in something called The Famous Pineville Junior High Arrow Pointing Toward Awesomeness Alignment. And that just wasn't acceptable.

"The Famous Pineville Junior High Arrow Pointing Toward Awesomeness Alignment is famous for a reason," Bethany said. "It's our signature alignment."

I'm not the sporty type, as a participant or a spectator. And having never attended a Pineville Junior High football game, I had no idea what The Famous Pineville Junior High Arrow Pointing Toward Awesomeness Alignment even was. For my sister's sanity, I tried to pretend otherwise.

"Right! Of course! The Awesome Arrow of...uh... Awesomeness?"

I could tell that my sister was about to give up at this point, so baffled was she by the notion that one could exist for twelve-almost-thirteen years and not know that The Famous Pineville Junior High Arrow Pointing Toward

Awesomeness Alignment is this: There are fourteen girls on the CHEER TEAM!!!! The two tallest are five feet six inches. They stand in the middle of the line. Then the rest of the squad lines up next to them in descending order: five feet five, five feet four, and so on until the five feet evens are on the ends. When lined up in such a fashion, the cheerleaders form an alignment that resembles an Arrow Pointing Toward Awesomeness.

Annalise Shapiro was supposed to fill the five-foot-four spot on one side.

"Now that spot is yours! You're a vital part of The Alignment." She blew on her hands. "I mean, without the five-foot-four spot, one side of The Alignment would go right from five foot five to five foot three and well, that just wouldn't work at all."

"But, Bethany, I…"

"How are your back handsprings? And your cartwheels? I mean, you can do a basic cartwheel, right?"

And then Bethany laughed like she was *born* doing cartwheels. Like she literally popped out of Mom, flipped head over feet, and landed right in the bassinet with a hearty "Goo-goo-go, Pineville!"

I cannot do a basic cartwheel. But when your perfect older sister is paying attention to you for the first time ever and keeping her attention depends on your ability to do a cartwheel, you assure her that yes, yes, of course you can do a cartwheel.

"Who can't do a cartwheel?" I asked, dripping with sarcasm.

And Bethany gave me an "I know, right?" roll of the eyes and a gentle punch to the shoulder and I swear I'd never felt closer to her in all my life. I wanted to make the moment last.

"By the way, where's today's mail?" she asked.

I knew our time was short. Bethany would be out the door and back to campus before I knew it. So as I showed her to the stack on the table, I told her all about the disaster of Woodshop and how the teacher is a nut and I'm the only girl in the class and he's determined to keep me there.

"That's fantastic!" Bethany said as she sorted through the pile.

"It is?"

"Seriously! Why would you want to switch out of a sweet situation like that? No competition! All the better for getting a head start on IT List number three: Pick your first boyfriend wisely."

I didn't even have time to object. The Woodshop boys aren't exactly my type. Not that I even *have* a type.

"Just don't wear those T-shirts," Bethany cautioned, putting the mail back down.

"To Woodshop? Or the tryout?"

It was getting very difficult to keep track of the big-sisterly wisdom when it came all at once like this.

"ANYWHERE."

"Why not? The bands are cool, right?"

"Ugh. I have no idea if those bands are cool."

Now I was really confused.

Bethany sighed wearily. "They are the last remnants of a relationship with a rock-and-roll boyfriend," she said. "I liked him. I hated the music."

The front door had shut behind her before I'd even thought to ask if he was the same boy from IT List #3: Pick your first boyfriend wisely.

Chapter Twelve

The next day I did as my sister told me and ditched the vintage tees in favor of one of the T-shirts Mom had picked out for me at the mall. In a slippery purple fabric with silvery stripes, this top was probably the show-offiest thing I owned. It won Bridget's approval right away.

"Don't get me wrong. I liked the vintage vibe you were going with," she said as we walked to the bus stop, "but this is more…"

"Me?" I asked, unconvinced. The shiny silver threads were kind of scratchy.

"More junior high," Bridget concluded.

Well, it must have been the right choice because the rest of the girls couldn't stop complimenting me on it either.

"Loving! Loving! Loving it!"

"So amazing!"

"Totally adorable fashion do!"

And so it's been for all the days that have followed since. Whenever I've worn something from the mall, I've gotten compliments. I think Sara, Manda, and Hope are all being sincere. But it's impossible not to notice that my adorable top had come from the same store as the adorable skirts Bridget and Sara had worn on the first day of school, and the same store as the adorable cardigan Hope was wearing today, and the same store as the adorable low-cut tank top Manda will probably wear tomorrow. By LOVING my AMAZING and TOTALLY ADORABLE FASHION DO, they were, in fact, complimenting themselves, too.

It's just one of the observations I've made about junior high so far.

Here's another observation: All the teachers seem to be under the mistaken impression that they are the only ones assigning homework. I mean, it's doable and all, but it's so much more than we used to get in elementary school! Take tonight, for example.

Language Arts: a five-paragraph essay describing our favorite character in *The Outsiders*. (I picked Ponyboy, which is kind of obvious because he's the narrator. He likes books and writing and thinks too much about things. Like me.)

Español: choosing the correct form of the verb *to be* in ten sentences. (Apparently there are two ways *to be* in Spanish. The *estar* way *to be* is temporary. The *ser* way *to be* is fixed. Too much of my life right now feels *estar*.)

Pre-Algebra: a worksheet about simplifying variable expressions. (The cool thing about math is that an answer is either right or wrong. It's one of the rare *ser* parts of my day.)

Physical Science: answering multiple-choice review questions for the first section of the first chapter of our textbook, *General Principles of Physical Science*. (Yes, it is as fascinating as it sounds. The most challenging part of this assignment is not drooling all over my textbook when I fall asleep.)

Social Studies: create a physical map for a new Earth. (Oh, that's not asking for too much, is it? On top of everything else? To CREATE A WHOLE NEW FREAKING PLANET?)

Woodshop: no homework. THIS IS THE ONLY GOOD THING ABOUT WOODSHOP.

Speaking of Woodshop, Mr. Pudel isn't the only junior high teacher who can't remember who any of us are. This is kind of understandable, though. In elementary school our teacher had pretty much the same twenty-five kids all day long. Here our teachers have a whole bunch of classes with twenty-five kids each. I'll be lucky if any of my teachers know my name before June. Unlike Mr. Pudel, most make an effort. After trying and failing to commit any of our names to memory in the first week, our Language Arts teacher decided to GET CREATIVE!

Language Arts teachers love to GET CREATIVE!

"Let's GET CREATIVE!" Miss Orden suggested after making the mistake of calling Manda "Sara." This error put Manda in a snit of overenunciation. I've noticed that Manda overenunciates whenever she's really annoyed but trying hard not to sound really annoyed.

"I. Don't. Look. Anything. Like. Sara."

And it was true. Physically she and Sara don't look anything alike. Most notably, Sara has corkscrew curly dark brown hair and Manda has flat-ironed dark blond hair. But in Miss Orden's defense, their outfits—sparkly top, flippy skirt—were essentially identical not only to each other, but to, oh, I don't know, about half of the seventh-grade female population.

Myself included.

So Miss Orden asked us all to reintroduce ourselves using an adjective that begins with the first letter of our first names.

"It's a mnemonic device," she said. "Do you know what that means?"

No one raised a hand. Miss Orden looked right at me. She had already figured out that I'd always give in to the awkward silence.

"A mnemonic device is a memory tool," I said.

"That's right! And what's your name again?" she asked.

"Jessica Darling," I replied, suddenly feeling the classroom's eyes on me.

"Well, I may not even need a mnemonic device to remember your name, but I'd like to hear one anyway!"

I had one ready to go. See, the reason I know the definition of *mnemonic* (as well as the fact that the *m* is silent so it's pronounced *nih-MON-ik*) is because we've been asked to play this particular name game several times over the years. I was stumped the first time, back in fourth grade. Think about it: There aren't a lot of obvious adjectives that start with *J*.

I ended up using *jazzy*, which was definitely not an accurate descriptor but was the first thing that popped into my head because it was the name of my pet gerbil that has since gone on to that great spinning wheel in the sky. And though she didn't mean to do it, Dori Sipowitz ended up totally embarrassing me by announcing, "Oh! You're Jazzy like the gerbil!" which led to me being followed around by the catchphrase "Jazzy like the gerbil" for the next month or two. Who knows? I could still be followed around by "Jazzy like the gerbil" if Dori hadn't peed herself at the Spring Choral Concert during the *Sound of Music* medley, which inevitably led to the new bullying catchphrase, "Do-Re-Mi! Do-ri PEE!"

Looking back now, I think that was probably the beginning of the end of 3ZNUF.

Anyway, the point is, I've been prepared with a *J*-adjective ever since.

"I'm Jessica," I announced to Miss Orden, "and I'm journalistic."

Predictably, Miss Orden loved that one. I wasn't trying to be the teacher's pet, but it was clear I was well on my way to becoming one. Then again, I didn't have much competition. My adjective of choice was way more impressive than:

"I'm Sara and I'm sweet!"

"I'm Hope and I'm hopeful."

(I think Hope was being intentionally lame, in which case that was pretty funny. But I really haven't figured her out yet, so I don't know if she was joking or what.)

And finally:

"I'm Manda and I'm mondo."

And everyone, including Miss Orden, was like, "What the heck?"

Which was exactly what Manda wanted.

"I'm mondo," she repeated as if we were the weird ones for not really knowing what she meant by that.

By lunchtime, it had become clear enough.

Manda said, "Your shoes are so mondo" to Sara.

Sara said, "Football boys are so mondo" to Bridget.

Bridget said, "So Burke Roy is mondo, right?" to us all.

Then right as the bell for eighth period rang, Hope said, "Burning your hand on the stove in Family and Consumer Sciences is so not mondo."

There you have it. One day in the not-so-distant future, when *mondo* is inducted alongside *awesome* and *sweet* into the Pineville Junior High Slang Hall of Fame, we will remember where we were the first time we heard it: seventh grade, first period, G&T Language Arts. More important, we'll remember it was Manda who said it.

Which—again—was exactly what Manda wanted.

In other classroom news, Mr. Pudel greeted our class with arm-swooping choreography worthy of a Broadway revue.

"*Beeeeee the treeeeee!*" he sang. "*Beeeeee the treeeeee!*"

Trust me, it was waaaaay weirder than Mom and Dad's first-day-of-school song and dance. It was the type of behavior I'd expect from a floaty goddess-of-poetry type like Miss Orden, not a Woodshop teacher built like a professional wrestler. Apparently, this song was meant to inspire us to get in touch with our "inner natural resources" because if we "respect the wood," we would be less likely to "waste the wood."

"Wasting the wood," Mr. Pudel warned, "is the worst thing you can do in this classroom."

Leave it to that redheaded kid Aleck to ask what I was thinking.

"Even worse than losing a finger?"

And then Mr. Pudel nonpointed at him with the empty space where his pointer finger would've been. You know? If he still had one.

"That won't happen," he said. "You've all passed the workshop safety exam."

This didn't make me feel any better. I assume Mr. Pudel had also passed the workshop safety exam at one point in his life. And yet he still lost a finger. In this very classroom. Doing exactly the sort of thing he was assuring us we were adequately prepared to do.

See, after a week's worth of woodshop safety videos, Mr. Pudel had determined that we were finally ready to "be the tree." Personally, I would've preferred spending the rest of the marking period taking multiple-choice workshop safety exams. Sample question:

1. Most workshop injuries occur when someone
    doesn't use:
    A. polite words like *please* and *thank you*
    B. deodorant
    C. COMMON SENSE!!!

I was in the minority, of course. The guys couldn't wait
to get their hands on the band saws, table saws, miter saws,
routers, lathes, and jointers—scary-sounding machinery
I'm only comfortable using within the context of multiple-
choice exams.

"Um, Mr. Pudel," I said.

"Yes, Clementine?"

Since he'd found out my last name was Darling, he had
taken to calling me Clementine. As in the cowpoke song
sung around a campfire. This was better than most of the
other nicknames he'd bestowed upon the boys, including
Mouth, Cheddar, and Squiggy. Even Aleck had really gotten off rather easy by comparison.

"Is there, like, another safety exam I could take?" I
began. "I'm not sure—"

Mr. Pudel cut me off. Like a finger.

"Class participation in the form of your completed
project is ninety percent of your grade, Clem. No spoon, no
passing this class."

So here's another multiple-choice question.

1. You're taking Woodshop. A class YOU'RE NOT SUPPOSED TO BE IN. You are required to use dangerous tools to carve a wooden spoon out of a block of soft maple. Do you...
   A. refuse, fail the class, and single-handedly sabotage your academic record?
   B. agree, and end up single handed?
   C. There is no third choice.

Sigh. I'm doomed to either fail Woodshop or lose a limb.

Chapter Thirteen

WAIT A SECOND. THERE'S ANOTHER UPSIDE TO WOODSHOP! If I lose a limb, I won't be able to try out for the CHEER TEAM!!!

HOORAY.

Who am I kidding? My handsprings couldn't possibly get any worse than they already are. Even without a *hand* to spring from.

Oh, did you think I'd forgotten all about #2 on the IT List? Unfortunately, my distraction strategy—Let's Think About Everything Else Except the Thing That Is Most on My Mind—could only work for so long. Especially when three of the other four girls at my lunch table also added their names to the sign-up sheet. Yes. Bridget, Manda, and Sara are also trying out for the CHEER TEAM!!!

Because Bridget has known me since birth, only she registered the reasonable response to seeing my name on the list.

"*You're* trying out for the CHEER TEAM!!!?" she asked with a gasp. "Why would you try out for the CHEER TEAM!!!?"

Four pairs of eyes scrutinized me from all around the lunch table. I didn't want to reveal the secret of the IT List. I wanted to keep it between Bethany and me. I tried another tactic instead of the truth.

"Uh. For the same reason all of you are trying out for the CHEER TEAM!!!"

"School spirit?" Bridget asked.

"Mondo uniforms?" Sara asked.

"Mondo boys?" Manda asked.

"Uh, yeah," I said. "Sure. All of the above."

Bridget, knowing me as she does, refused to let it drop.

"You can barely do a forward roll!" she protested. "When 3ZNUF used to play Olympic Gymnastics Team, you were always the scary Eastern European coach who yelled at us!"

Usually Manda pretended not to hear anything Bridget said. But this caught her interest.

"What's 3ZNUF?" she asked.

"Oh! That's the name Jess, our old friend Dor—OUCH!"

94

I kicked Bridget under the table to stop her from telling everyone that we used to be BFFs with Dori Sipowitz. I quickly changed the subject.

"So, Hope! Why aren't *you* trying out for the CHEER TEAM!!!?"

Hope looked up from her notebook. "Uh, what?"

She was too busy doodling portraits of all our teachers to pay the least bit of attention to our conversation. Her rendering of Mr. Odd's Frankenstein-square head was impressively lifelike.

"Why aren't you trying out for the CHEER TEAM!!!?"

"Yes, Hope," Manda chimed in. "Please tell us why you're totally bailing on our all-for-one-one-for-all promise to try out for the CHEER TEAM!!!?"

I'd no idea that Manda, Sara, and Hope had made such a promise. Or when. All I knew was that I hadn't been included in the pact.

Hope sighed and set down her pencil.

"I'm just not CHEER TEAM!!! material."

Then she picked up her pencil and started shading the shadows under Mr. Odd's bloodshot eyeballs.

"But you *promised* you would," Manda pressed.

Sara backed her up. "Omigod! You totally did."

And then the bell rang before this debate could go any further. I didn't have time to say it then, but I'll say it now:

Hope is getting more interesting by the day. Unfortunately, I don't think she feels the same way about me.

Anyway, Bridget wouldn't drop the subject on the bus ride home.

"Are your parents making you try out for the CHEER TEAM!!!?"

"Why would you ask that?"

Truth was, I knew exactly why she would ask that. Bridget knows my parents well. She wouldn't be surprised that they had, in fact, already given me an ultimatum: *Choose an extracurricular activity or we will choose one for you.*

"Because you and the CHEER TEAM!!! go together like…" She pulled on the ends of her hair as if switching on the lightbulb in her brain. "Like Cap'n Crunch and milk!"

This was an inside joke. Only Bridget knows I prefer eating my sugary cereals in overflowing handfuls, dry, right out of the box.

"So the best I can figure," she continued, "is that, like, your parents are forcing you to try out for the CHEER TEAM!!! because, like, that's what your sister did in junior high and they figure it's, like, what all girls do when they get to junior high."

Mom and Dad had absolutely no idea I was trying out for the CHEER TEAM!!! And it's highly doubtful that the CHEER TEAM!!! would be on their list of "approved" activities to choose from. Especially Dad. He blames one too many falls from the top of the pyramid for Bethany's below-average academic performance over the years.

Bridget leaned toward me, eyes wide and expectant, waiting for me to confirm her theory. I didn't want to lie to her, but I didn't want to tell her the truth either. Unlike the IT List, Bridget's explanation actually made some sense.

"Yes," I replied. "It's all my parents' fault."

Putting the blame on my parents was so perfectly logical that it was actually *better* than the truth.

That's what I told myself anyway.

I should've known that Bridget wouldn't be able to leave the discussion on the bus. Later that afternoon, I was in the hammock dozing off to *General Principles of Physical Science*, enjoying the last bit of mid-September Indian summer sunshine, when I was nearly startled to death by a shrieking *TWEEEEEEEET!*

I landed on the ground, looked up, and saw Bridget towering over me. Her legs were set in V-stance and her balled-up hands were pressed to her hips. She had stuffed her hair under a baseball cap and affixed a bushy black mustache to her upper lip.

TWEEEEEEEET!

She spit out the silver whistle and started yelling at me.

"YOU VANT TO BE ON CHEER TEAM!!! YOU VERK TO BE ON CHEER TEAM!!!"

Aha. Bridget had taken on the role of scary Eastern European coach. I was the inexperienced gymnast she would mold into gold-medal material. The big difference between Bridget and me was that she could actually execute all the stunts she was challenging me to do.

"YOU DO BACKTUCK. LIKE DEES?"

Then Bridget effortlessly flipped herself backward through the air and landed on her own two feet.

I shook my head.

"YOU DO AERIAL. LIKE DEES?"

Then Bridget spun into a hands-free cartwheel. The baseball cap didn't move. Nor did the mustache. How could she make something so impossible look so easy?

Again, I shook my head. *No way.*

"YOU DO … AH … DEE TOE TOUCH? LIKE DEES?"

Bridget jumped into a midair split and reached for the tips of her sneakers.

I didn't shake my head this time. I just kind of glared skeptically.

"Come on, Jess," Bridget said in her normal voice. "How are you gonna try out in front of a room full of strangers if you won't even, like, *try* in front of your best friend?"

She had a very valid point. But before I could give her any credit for it, she was already back to barking orders at me.

"YOU DO DEE TOE TOUCH. LIKE DEES."

It wasn't a question. It was a command.

"Okay," I relented. "I'll try the toe touch."

So I tried the toe touch. And I crashed onto the grass and nearly cracked my head open. Even the ever-optimistic Bridget had begun to accept my limitations.

"You're too tall to be a flier anyway," she reasoned. "Maybe you can be a base."

"A base?"

"The girls at the bottom of all the stunts."

That didn't sound like too much fun at all. It must have shown on my face because Bridget was quick to point out the importance of being a base.

"Sure, the fliers get all the glory," she said. "But without the bases, there wouldn't be any stunts for the fliers to do."

So we tested my base potential. Bridget tried to climb up onto my shoulders using my legs and arms like rungs on a ladder. I Weeble-wobbled and tried to keep my balance. This stunt-in-the-making resulted in yet another grass-smacking, head-cracking tumble, only this time Bridget added injury to injury by landing right on top of me. At this point, Bridget was over it.

"Your parents are crazy," she snapped, rubbing her elbow where it had gouged me in the rib cage. "Do they know you're not just risking your life, but the life of every girl on the squad?"

I hadn't really thought about it that way. And Bridget was looking so serious that I was a millisecond away from fessing up about Bethany's IT List and the real reason I was trying out for the CHEER TEAM!!! But Bridget never stayed upset for very long. She once said her parents' divorce taught her what's legitimately worth getting upset about. Everything else is no big whoop. Sure enough, within a few seconds she was grinning at me again.

"That's enough practice! You'll be awesome, Jess! I just know it! You've always been mondo at everything!"

First of all, I've never been *mondo* at everything because Manda just made up that word. Second, Bridget has seen me "dribble" a basketball, heard me "play" clarinet, and tasted my "brownies." I can't decide if she's my most loyal friend or my most delusional friend.

Probably both.

"VIGOROUS VERKOUT DESERVE REVESHMENT!"

Bridget half unzipped her BMB backpack just enough for me to see that it contained a fresh box of Cap'n Crunch and two bottles of Coke. With a whoop of glee, we ran upstairs to my bedroom, where we could sit on the rug and enjoy a junk food picnic in peace. Meaning, without my mother ranting against chemical additives and artificial flavors and all the things that make junk food taste so delicious.

We unscrewed our caps. The sodas made a satisfying whooshy fizzy noise.

"Cheers!" I said, tapping my bottle against hers.

"CHEERS!!!" Bridget shouted back. "And we're trying out for the CHEER TEAM!!! Freaky!"

It really wasn't freaky at all. We always said *cheers* during our junk food picnics. But Bridget seemed to enjoy thinking this toast had some cosmic significance and I didn't want to spoil her mood.

"What are you gonna say tonight at dinner when your mom asks why you aren't eating?" Bridget asked as she peeled off her fake mustache.

"I'll just tell her I am too full of her 'wonderful' granola bars and 'flavorful' seltzer."

Bridget laughed. I was definitely full of *something*, that's for sure.

Then all of a sudden Bridget got quiet, and the munching of cereal became the only sound. When her ears turned pink, I was afraid she was going to start talking about her mom and dad. Uh-oh. I didn't think I had it in me to be the positive pep-talker this afternoon. But it turns out that she had something else on her mind. Something that was even more impossible for me to talk about than her parents' divorce.

"So!" she said, clapping her hands and sending cereal crumbs through the air. "Who do you like?"

This was not at all what I had expected.

"Who do I like?" I repeated dumbly.

"Yeah, like." She paused. "Who. Do. You. Like?"

She asked the question slowly, as if we didn't speak the same language.

"Well," I began, "I guess I like Manda and Sara. They've been pretty nice to me so far. And I'm still getting to know Ho—"

Bridget playfully swatted my arm.

"Not other girls, silly!" She giggled. "BOYS! What boys do you like?"

She said it so matter-of-factly. Like there was no room for debate. There had to be not just one boy, but *boys plural* that I liked.

"Um," I stammered. "I don't know...."

Bridget gestured for me to come closer.

"Can you keep a secret?" she whispered.

I nodded, relieved that Bridget no longer seemed interested in discussing my hypothetical crushes. Luckily for me, she wanted this to be less of a conversation about the boys I liked and more about the one very specific boy she liked.

"I think I like Burke Roy!" she said, squeezing her arms around herself in a dangerously tight hug. "And I think he likes me!"

Now, I've already made it pretty clear that I know very little about boy/girl business. And yet, even to my innocent eyes, it was clear that Burke had it bad for Bridget. And vice versa. So the only thing I could say to Bridget was this:

"No duh!"

This was not the appropriate response. Her face fell.

"No duh what part?" she asked anxiously. "No duh that I like him or no duh that he likes me? Because if it's so obvious that I like him and he doesn't like me that would be, like, so incredibly embarrassing because he's, like, this totally popular eighth grader and I'm just this pathetic puppy dog of a seventh grader...."

Her whole face had turned as red as a stop sign. And that's what I needed to make her do.

"STOP!" I shouted. "Calm down!"

Bridget just kind of wheezed for a few seconds. It was like she had worked herself into preteen cardiac arrest.

"I meant, 'no duh' to all of it," I said. "He's obviously liked you since the first day of school. And you obviously like him because..."

Why did Bridget like him anyway? Because he was a cute football player? Was that all that mattered? Did she know anything else about him? Had they ever had a conversation? Or did he communicate solely through impressive armpit fart noises?

"I like him because he's Burke Roy!" Bridget squealed. "He's hot and popular and a football player. Who wouldn't like him?"

"I don't like him," I said automatically.

Bridget cocked her head to the side.

"Yeah, but that's only because you knew I liked him and you're such a bestie that you would never like someone who I was interested in because that breaks all the rules of best friendship! Otherwise you would totally have the hots for him because who wouldn't?"

I had a feeling that denying this bogus accusation would only make Bridget feel bad for some reason. I just let her think it by saying nothing at all. This was okay, I guess, because for the next half hour Bridget talked enough for the both of us without actually adding anything new or interesting to the conversation.

"So I think I like him and I think he likes me, which is just, you know, wow, because he's so hot and popular and a football player and I'm just, like, me, a little seventh grader and do you think he knows I like him and do you think he knows I know he might like me back?"

See what I mean?

She'd probably still be going on about Burke Roy if my mom hadn't knocked on my door.

"Hellooooo? Girls?"

I'm so glad I had the door locked. We quickly stashed the cereal box and sodas under my bed before letting her in.

"Hey, Mom!"

"Hey, Mrs. Darling!"

My mother sniffed the air, suspicious. I swear, to my fitness-obsessed mother, Cap'n Crunch and Coke are no better than booze and cigarettes.

"Bridget, would you like to stay for dinner?" my mom asked, still looking around the room for a sign to confirm her vague suspicion of rule breaking. "It's kale casserole night!"

I have to credit Bridget for not gagging right in my mother's face.

"Thanks, Mrs. Darling," Bridget replied, "but there's a microwave burrito at home with my name on it."

Mom did her best to turn her disapproving grimace into a smile.

"Well, you know you're welcome here anytime."

Bridget thanked my mom and leaped to her feet. Then she offered one last bit of coaching before departing.

"When in doubt, Jess," she said, "just smile, smile, smile!"

As Bridget bopped past her, Mom regarded her with something close to awe. She waited until Bridget was out of earshot before speaking.

"What a wonderful philosophy despite everything she's gone through," Mom said.

It's true. For Bridget, putting on a happy face went well beyond the CHEER TEAM!!! tryouts. It was her life's mission. But how often had Bridget's sunshiny personality blinded me to the darker moods lurking beneath the surface?

Blinded everyone?

"Maybe *you* could benefit from such an attitude adjustment," Mom suggested. "Have you noticed Bridget's skin lately? She's glowing!"

And before I could reply, Mom not-so-gently poked at my chin.

"Ouch!"

I rubbed the small, swollen bump I hadn't been aware of until Mom literally pointed it out to me.

"Maybe if you were more positive like Bridget, you wouldn't have pimples."

As she headed back downstairs, I couldn't help but think that my mom had it all backward.

Maybe if I were less pimply like Bridget, I'd be more positive.

Chapter Fourteen

CHEER TEAM!!! tryouts are tomorrow. But that didn't stop major drama from going down today.

"Omigod!" Sara cried out when she saw me at our lockers before homeroom. "Where's your cheer flair?"

Until that moment, I had never heard the term *cheer flair*. But one look at Sara and I knew exactly what she was referring to. She was decked out in red, white, and blue Pineville Junior High paraphernalia from the shiny bow in her hair to the sparkly shoelaces on her sneakers. In addition to her standard makeup job, she had a dancing chicken painted on her face.

"Nice chicken," I said, pointing to her cheek.

"Duh! It's not a chicken!" she snapped. "It's our school mascot!"

Oops. I guess I should've known that.

"Ohhh. I totally see it now!" I said. "Flighty the Seagull."

"*Mighty* the Seagull! Don't you know anything? And where's your cheer flair? Manda said we're all wearing our cheer flair!"

Like I said, I never knew there was such a thing as cheer flair until about thirty seconds earlier in this conversation. Sara was too worried about herself to wait for an answer. She sneered at the offending bird in her magnetic locker mirror, then spit on a tissue and furiously rubbed her cheek. This didn't remove the bird so much as just smear it from forehead to chin, which made Sara even angrier.

"Omigod! Omigod! Omigod!"

That's when Sara ran to tell our teacher to mark her "present" and that she would be unable to attend homeroom because she needed to go to the bathroom to deal with "girl stuff." And by that Sara meant going down the hall to the WXYZ homeroom to drag Weaver, Hope out of class and into the bathroom to fix her face.

Hope worked her artistic magic, all right. When Sara came strutting into first period, there was an exact copy of Mighty the Seagull where the funky chicken used to be.

"Good save," I said to Hope.

"Don't congratulate me yet," she replied drily.

And before I could ask what she was talking about, Manda sashayed into the room.

"Sara!" she said in a chipper way that sounded rehearsed. "Your cheer flair is so mondo."

Manda was conspicuously free of cheer flair.

"Omigod! Manda!" Sara screeched. "Where's *your* cheer flair?"

Manda widened her eyes in innocence. "You didn't get my message?"

"What message?" Sara asked through gritted teeth. Her cheek bulged every time her jaw clenched, making it look like Mighty the Seagull was flexing his feathery muscles.

"The message," Manda continued, "where I said that it was a bad idea to wear our cheer flair today to psych out the competition because then everyone would totally copy us at tryouts tomorrow so it was way smarter to wait until *right* before tryouts so we stand out from everyone else. That message?"

Then Manda made a point of winking at me, as if we were in on this together.

"Omigod! So Jessica got your message and I didn't?"

"I didn't get any message about anything!" I protested.

"Then why am I the only fool walking around school with a dancing chicken on my cheek?!?"

"Seagull," Hope and I said at the same time. Our

spontaneous simultaneous response gave us the giggles. This was not an acceptable reaction.

"HAHAHA. EVERYONE LAUGH AT SARA. HAHA-HAHA. OMIGOD, I HATE YOU ALL."

Manda closed her eyes and rubbed her temples as if this conversation were giving her the huuuuugest headache ever.

"Puh-leeze, Sara," Manda said dismissively. "You're so paranoid."

As Manda and Sara bickered about which of Sara's many communication devices Manda had allegedly messaged, Hope rolled her eyes and gave me a "what can you do?" shrug.

"Did you know Manda had tricked her?" I whispered to her.

She glanced at their standoff and sighed knowingly.

"No, but I knew one of them would do *something* to psych out the other. I guarantee that Sara will wear her flair all day just so Manda doesn't have the satisfaction of seeing her take it off. Some BFFs, huh?"

I thought about how Bridget had gone out of her way to coach me and encourage me and how lucky I was to have her in my life. I wonder if Hope has anyone like that in hers.

So Manda and Sara only spoke to each other through

dirty looks the rest of the day. I'm sure they'd still be giving each other the silent treatment if they hadn't been brought back together through a common enemy.

"Omigod!" Sara gasped as she slammed down her lunch tray. "Guess who's trying out for the CHEER TEAM!!!?"

There was no question to whom this question was being addressed.

"Who's trying out for the CHEER TEAM!!!?" Manda asked. She tried to sound bored, but I could tell she cared very much about this information. She hated when Sara knew something she didn't.

"Dori Sipowitz!"

My jaw dropped, though I didn't know why. Back in the 3ZNUF days, Dori was an even better gymnast than Bridget. CHEER TEAM!!! made sense.

"How do you know that?" I asked.

"Duh! I checked the list! She must have just added her name!"

Manda was unfazed by Sara's gossip.

"Who's Dori Sipowitz and why should I care?"

Bridget had arrived at the table just in time to hear Manda ask this question.

"Dori Sipowitz?"

Bridget asked this as if she hadn't said that name in years. Because she hadn't.

"Dori Sipowitz."

Like her post-orthodontic smile, once Bridget started saying Dori Sipowitz, she couldn't stop.

"What about Dori Sipowitz? Does Dori Sipowitz go to this school? I didn't even know Dori Sipowitz went to this school!"

That's how invisible Dori Sipowitz was at Pineville Junior High School. She'd been in the same lunch period as Bridget for more than two weeks and her former best friend hadn't even noticed.

"Jess, did you know Dori Sipowitz went to this school?"

I shrugged sheepishly. This turned out to be a sufficient answer because Sara was in full tell-all mode. Sara hadn't acknowledged Dori's existence since cutting her on the lunch line on day one. So I didn't know *when* Sara bothered to learn Dori's name, but I knew *why*. In the two weeks since we met in homeroom, I'd come to realize that Sara was a girl who lived for gossip about everything and everyone—even someone as insignificant as Dori Sipowitz—because she never knew when that information could be useful later on.

"Dori sits with that other Not at the square tables! Near the kitchen!" Sara rounded on Manda. "And *that's* why you should care!"

This was all Manda needed to hear.

"Square tables! Near the kitchen! That Not thinks she's cheer material? Puh-leeze."

"Omigod," Sara agreed. "I know."

As Manda and Sara debated the attributes that makes one "cheer material" (not sitting at the square tables near the kitchen FOR SURE), Hope caught my eye.

"Bee-Eff-Effs," she mouthed.

Hope made me laugh for the second time this entire nerve-racking, nauseating day.

"There!" Sara shouted as if she had just spotted a wilde-beest. "She's right there!"

And all our heads swiveled toward the square tables near the kitchen.

"The one who looks like a 'before' photo?" Manda cracked.

As much as I hated to admit it, Dori did kind of resemble a classic makeover candidate. She had limp brown hair and wore no makeup. And she seemed to care even less about fashion than I did, favoring sweaters hand-knit by her grandma that overwhelmed her tiny frame. But with her flawless complexion and piercing green eyes, Dori was nowhere near ugly. She was just, um…pre-pretty.

"Sheesh! She's right!" Bridget slapped her hand to her forehead. "That's Dori Sipowitz! I hadn't even noticed her!"

No one notices grape jelly.

"She must think I'm the worst friend ever! We have

to say hello!" Bridget was already up and on her way over. "3ZNUF! 4EVA!"

Now this was just too much for Manda and Sara to handle.

"Three zee wha?" they asked each other.

"Jess! Come on!"

Bridget bopped up and down with impatience. Her cute little move drew applause from the nearby table of football players. Burke Roy led the fist-pumping chant.

"Bee-Em-Bee! Bee-Em-Bee!"

She spun around to face them. Gone were the days when Bridget was totally oblivious to the boys' mating calls.

"Sheeeeeeeesh!" Bridget squealed. "You guuuuuuuys!" She made a point to swat Burke Roy extra hard on the shoulder.

This distraction was all it took for Manda and Sara to get a jump on the Dori Sipowitz situation.

"Come on, girls," Manda said. "Let's wish Dori luck!"

Notice she didn't specify what *kind* of luck.

Sara didn't hesitate. "Omigod! Totally!"

The two of them stood side by side and stared down me and Hope.

"So?"

Hope barely looked up from her doodles.

"This is cheer business," she said. "I'm out."

That left me. Alone.

"You heard her," Manda said. "This is cheer business."

"Come *onnnnn*," Sara whined.

It was a nastily accurate imitation of Bridget, who had totally forgotten about Dori Sipowitz and was now removing the PJHS baseball cap that Burke Roy had pulled down over her eyes.

"Come *onnnnnn.* . . ."

I tried to reason with Manda and Sara.

"It can't really be cheer business when we're not even on the team. . . ."

"Yet!" Manda and Sara said at the same time.

Then these two girls who HATED EACH OTHER ALL DAY high-fived because they were so in sync.

"Bee-Eff-Effs!"

Ack.

I cast a quick glance at Dori. She was animatedly telling her friend a story as she zipped up her lunch tote. I bet she brought her lunch every day to avoid the whole cafeteria line-cutting pecking order. That's why I was a bringer. And though I didn't know for sure, I'm willing to bet it's why Hope was a bringer, too.

Manda and Sara were tap-tap-tapping their feet, keeping a furious tempo.

"Comonnnnnnn...."

I wish I could say that this was when I grew a backbone. When I stood tall and strong enough to say, *Hey, Dori doesn't deserve to be psyched out before tryouts just because you don't like her, which is stupid because you've never even met her and the thing is that I actually do know her and she's supernice if, okay, a little boring, but you know what? That's not even fair for me to say—maybe she isn't boring anymore—but I have no idea because I haven't bothered to get to know her again, which almost—almost—makes me as judgmental as you two are....*

And maybe I would have. I'd like to think I would have. But I was saved by the eighth-period bell.

Dori was saved, too. She was already out the door before Manda and Sara had an opportunity to prey upon her vulnerability.

I was gathering up my stuff when Hope tapped me on the shoulder and asked a simple yet complex question.

"Why?"

There were a bazillion questions within that three-letter word. *Why are you trying out for the CHEER TEAM!!!?* was the most obvious and with the most straightforward answer. (IT List #2: Make the CHEER TEAM!!!) Others included: *Why am I friends with these girls?* (IT List #4: Stick with the IT clique.) *Why am I watching Bridget flirt* with Burke? (IT List #3: Pick your first boyfriend wisely.) *Why did I borrow this shirt from Bridget even though it keeps riding up because my torso is way too long?* (IT List #1: Wear something different every day.)

And yet, at that moment, the answer I actually gave Hope also could have served as the correct response to the most common question I'd been asking myself since the last day of summer: *Why does Bethany's IT List matter so much to me?*

"Why?" Hope repeated when I didn't say anything right away.

"I don't know," I said finally. "I just don't know."

Chapter Fifteen

Ack.

Not even Bridget could put a positive spin on my CHEER TEAM!!! tryout. Let's put it this way: Losing my hand in Woodshop would have been less traumatizing than what just happened in the gym.

This is one of those stories where the teller is like, "You don't want to hear this story," and the listener is like, "Of course I want to hear the story," and the teller is like, "Seriously, you don't want to hear this story because it's a terrible story where terrible things happen," and the listener is like, "I REALLY WANT TO HEAR THIS STORY SO JUST TELL ME THE STORY," and the teller is like, "Fine, I will," and tells the story and when it's all over the listener is superdepressed and like, "Wow, I wish you hadn't told me that terrible story," and the teller is like, "See? I told you so," but doesn't feel very good about it.

And yet, part of me thinks that by telling the terrible, traumatizing tale of CHEER TEAM!!! tryouts, I might be less haunted by its memory for years to come.

I certainly can't imagine feeling any worse about it than I already do.

So. Here it goes.

The day started out okay. Bridget offered me more last-minute tips on the bus to school.

"I believe you're a base! You have to believe it, too!"

It was nice to know that there was one person in the world who believed in me so completely. Even if such believing was of the Tooth Fairy/Easter Bunny variety. I was reminded of Mr. Pudel's inspirational song.

"Beeeeee the base," I sang to Bridget. *"Beeeeee the base."*

I expected Bridget to laugh, or even to sing along with me. So I was taken by surprise when she ducked low and yanked me down with her.

"Shhhhhhh!" Bridget hissed.

"Ouch! I need that arm!"

I was annoyed and yet I still couldn't help but think that a broken arm would be a valid excuse for not participating in the CHEER TEAM!!! Or Woodshop, for that matter.

"Shhhh! Burke Roy might hear you! And that would be, like, so embarrassing!"

This coming from a girl who recently showed up at my house in a fake mustache and shouted at me in a bad Eastern European accent? I almost said as much, but that's when Bridget popped her head back up and gave Burke Roy a cheery little wave that—I don't know—made me feel... well...pretty darn cheerless, which is not a good way to feel on the day you're trying out for the CHEER TEAM!!!

So I got off the bus and spent the next eight periods trying not to puke.

No matter how hard Manda and Sara tried to project coolness, they were obviously as nervous as I was. Manda put so much effort into forcing a smile on her face that she looked like an insane jack-o'-lantern. And Sara only spoke when called on in class. I honestly didn't think Sara was capable of keeping her mouth shut for eight seconds let alone eight classes. And when Bridget and Dori Sipowitz didn't show up for lunch, I assumed that it had something to do with them being freaked out about tryouts, too.

I didn't find Bridget and couldn't persuade Manda and Sara to speed up their primping in the locker room, so I went to the tryouts alone. The gym was full of restless ponytailed girls—some I sort of recognized, but mostly not—eager to get started and get done. They burned off their nervous energy by walking on their hands or jumping into full splits, you know, just mindlessly doing amazing things with their bodies that I could never, ever do in a bazillion years.

"Jess!"

I was so relieved to hear Bridget's familiar voice, but I couldn't find her in the crowd. The next thing I knew, she and another blur of a girl were cartwheeling, roundoffing, handspringing right at me. They landed in sync.

"3ZNUF!" Bridget chanted. "4EVA!"

Dori smiled shyly at me.

"Hey, Dori," I said, still embarrassed by that first-day-of-school line cut.

"Sheesh, Jess! Dori is an even better gymnast than I remembered! We skipped lunch because she asked me to coach her before tryouts, but I was the one who really needed coaching!"

"You're mondo," Dori said to Bridget.

"No, you're mondo!" Bridget said to Dori.

"No. Seriously. *You're* mondo."

And I was like, *MONDO* ISN'T EVEN A REAL WORD.

"Hello, ladies!" a peppy voice cut through the chatter. "I'm Miss Garcia!"

Aha. My sister's friend. The girls in the gym went, "Whoooooooo!"

"Welcome to Pineville Junior High CHEER TEAM!!! tryouts!"

We all *Whoooooooooed!* again.

Miss Garcia had a girlish, almost childlike voice. And yet she effortlessly commanded our attention without a microphone or even a megaphone.

She started a chant.

"WHO'S A-W-E?" *[clap clap]* "S-O-M-E?" *[stomp stomp]*

Every girl in that gym knew what to do.

"AWE-SOME." *[stomp stomp]*

"AWE-SOME." *[clap clap]*

"AWE-SOME ARE WE." *[stomp-clap, stomp-clap]*

Every girl knew to do this. Except me. I just stood there like a slack-limbed dummy.

Then Miss Garcia did a bazillion flips to get from one side of the gym to the other. Apparently, this is a cheerleader's favorite method of getting from one place to another. All the girls *Whoooed* again. Miss Garcia stuck the landing and gently patted her slicked-back ponytail. Not a single strand of glossy black hair was out of place.

"The word *awesome* means 'to inspire awe,'" Miss Garcia said, clutching her fist to her chest. "And that's what we do here on the CHEER TEAM!!! We make the impossible possible!"

As I looked around the room and saw Bridget's and Dori's and everyone else's enraptured faces, it hit me: WHAT THE HECK WAS I DOING HERE?

The only thing more ridiculous than the IT List was my determination to follow it! Why couldn't I just explain to Bethany that I wasn't cheer material? The answer came easily. I couldn't tell the truth because my sister would be disappointed by my dorkiness and go back to showing zero interest in my life.

I didn't want that.

"We turn losers into winners!" Miss Garcia continued.

I also really, really didn't want to try out for the CHEER TEAM!!! And even if I did muster the courage to go through with it, there was no way I was actually going to make it. Not with so many more twisty, bendy, perky girls to choose from.

"Dreamers into doers..."

I had to get out of there. And I'd almost inched my way to the exit without Miss Garcia or Bridget or anyone else noticing when the exit doors sprung open and slammed against the walls with a "look at us" *BANG*!

Manda and Sara were making their grand entrance.

While the rest of us were dressed in gym shorts and

Pineville Junior High T-shirts as instructed, Manda and Sara were head to toe bedazzled in Pineville Junior High's patriotic colors. Cheerleaders aren't known for their subtlety, but there was waaaay too much red, white, and blue going on. It was like the Statue of Liberty and Uncle Sam had a baby and that baby barfed stars and stripes all over them.

So much for slipping out unnoticed. Miss Garcia came to an abrupt stop and pointed at Manda and Sara.

"Five laps."

The sweetness in her voice was tinged with something else.

"*Now.*"

Poison.

Manda and Sara looked at each other, then looked around the room like, "What?"

"*You* and *you*," said Miss Garcia. "Five minutes late. Five laps."

And I honestly didn't know if it was out of nervousness or obnoxiousness or what, but getting reprimanded in front of everyone made Manda and Sara laugh out loud. In an instant, Miss Garcia hustled over and got right in their faces.

"What are your names?"

Manda and Sara stopped laughing and told her their names.

"Well, Manda Powers and Sara D'Abruzzi," Miss Garcia said, "you are dismissed."

Manda and Sara laughed again. Until they realized that they were the only ones laughing.

"Puh-leeze," Manda said. "You're kidding, right?"

Miss Garcia said nothing.

"Omigod!" Sara yelped. "But we're barely even late! And the only reason we were barely even late is because well—duh!—check out all this mondo cheer flair! You don't see anyone else rocking so much cheer flair!"

"And I don't see anyone else wasting my time either," Miss Garcia replied before turning her back on them and returning to the middle of the room. "Now where was I?" she asked aloud. The poison in her voice was gone. It was pure sugar. "Oh yes! We turn chumps into champs...."

And when it was clear to Manda and Sara that no amount of huffing and puffing would make Miss Garcia change her mind, they stormed out of the auditorium, leaving a trail of red, white, and blue glitter in their wake.

Bridget had found me again, and nudged me in the side.

"Whoa," she mouthed, too intimidated to say it aloud.

Okay. I know what you're thinking. You're thinking, *Jessica, you lied! This isn't a terrible story at all! What's there not to like about this story?*

The terrible part of the story happened right after Sara and Manda were ejected, when Miss Garcia scanned the crowd and pointed a finger in my direction.

"You!" she said, perkier than ever. "You're Bethany Darling's sister! I'd recognize that special cheeritude anywhere!"

I'd already felt weird about having inside information about the Awesome Arrow or whatever it was. Now Miss Garcia was singling me out? I didn't want this special treatment!

"Uh," I stammered. "Yeah. I—"

Miss Garcia flinched. "No! Not you! The blonde!"

It was clear now that Miss Garcia wasn't pointing at me after all.

"*She's* a mini Bethany and future CHEER TEAM!!! captain if I ever saw one!"

She was pointing at Bridget.

"Sheesh! I'm so flattered!" Bridget's cheeks burned red. "But I'm not Bethany's sister!"

Then, in a move I might never forgive her for, she pushed me forward.

"*This* is Bethany's sister! Jessica Darling!"

It lasted a millisecond, maybe. But I saw it. The look of disappointment followed by the look of someone trying to cover up her disappointment.

"Oh! *You're* Jessica!" Miss Garcia gushed. "I see the resemblance!"

She did not see the resemblance. No one has ever seen the resemblance. It's never really bothered me before, but it did then. Maybe because it was the first time someone *had* seen the gorgeous resemblance between my sister and my best friend.

Miss Garcia gestured for me to come forward. I felt like my sneakers were filled with cement.

"Show us what you've got!"

Bridget gave me an enthusiastic thumbs-up.

"Show us what you've got!"

Miss Garcia sure knew how to pump up a crowd. Almost instantly, the gym came alive with the chant.

"Show us what you've got!" *[clap clap, clap clap]*

Here's the thing: The encouragement was strangely contagious. I know it sounds crazy, but my confidence soared at the sound of their cheers. Miss Garcia's speech suddenly made perfect sense. Cheering made the impossible possible! Turned losers into winners! Dreamers into doers! Chumps into champs!

"SHOW US WHAT YOU'VE GOT!" *[clap clap, clap clap]*

I made my way to the end of the floor mat and prepared myself to show them what I had. Whatever that was.

Which, as it turns out, wasn't very much.

So what was I thinking in these last moments before the disaster?

I had this idea that it might be helpful to approach my stunt according to *General Principles of Physical Science*. Maybe I could harness what my *brain* knew about motion, mass, and momentum into something my *body* could know, too. And with that mind-body knowledge, I'd execute the perfect aerial cartwheel on my first-ever attempt!

"Physical Science, don't fail me now," I whispered to myself before running across the mat, pushing off on the balls of my feet, propelling myself into the air . . .

WHAM!

Fireworks in my eyes. Bells in my ears. Blood in my nose.

The most spectacular, Olympic-level face flop of all time.

Silence. Pin-drop silence.

Followed by peals of laughter.

Bridget and Dori were the only ones who didn't laugh. Everyone else laughed. My only small consolation was that Manda and Sara weren't there to see it for themselves. I would have never heard the end of it.

Miss Garcia didn't waste any time. She brusquely looked me over and determined that the only permanent damage I'd done was to my pride. She told Bridget and Dori to pull me to my feet and efficiently whipped out a tape measure.

"Five foot four," she murmured. "And a *quarter.*"

I'd forgotten to slouch. Just a squinch.

I didn't want Bridget and Dori to miss their tryouts on my account. I refused their offer to escort me back to the locker room.

Miss Garcia didn't have to tell me I was dismissed. That I wasn't cheer material was painfully obvious. Ha. In more ways than one.

Chapter Sixteen

You're not going to believe this because I definitely didn't: I MADE THE ***CHEER TEAM!!!*** (Yes, I've added ***asterisks*** to that announcement. I'll get around to that.)

So I was lying on my bed, icing my floor-flattened face with a bag of frozen edamame, when I heard noises down-stairs. My parents were both out of the house—Dad on his bike, Mom at her office—so I dragged myself downstairs to see what was going on. This was the last thing I felt like doing because in the kitchen—just as I'd feared—was the last person I felt like seeing. Honestly, I would have been happier if I'd stumbled upon my friendly neighborhood ax murderer.

"Congratulations!" Bethany squealed as she wrapped me in a hug. "You did it!"

"Uh. Did what?" Humiliate myself? Break my face?

"*Did what?*" Bethany said in imitation. "So modest! Sherri—Miss Garcia—called! She's thrilled to offer you a special spot on the team!"

I swear if she had said, "The president of the United States called. He's thrilled to offer you a special spot on his superawesome secret spy team," I would have been less surprised.

"Uh—what?"

"She thanked me for alerting her to your special talents!" she said. "And perfect timing, too! She called when I was already on my way over here!"

Aha. Bethany hadn't made a special trip just to congratulate me after all. She had another reason for being here while my parents were out. And sure enough, she headed straight for the mail on the kitchen counter. As she'd done before, she sifted through it, clearly looking for something specific.

"What are you looking for?" I asked.

She froze. "What do you mean?"

"You come to the house when you know Mom and Dad are out of the house—usually on a Tuesday, now that I think about it. You make small talk, search through the mail, then leave. You're looking for something. What are you looking for?"

Bethany's mouth tightened for a moment, then loosened up into a half smile.

"Can you keep a secret?" she whispered even though we were alone.

My sister was asking me to keep a secret. I'm usually the one she keeps secrets from! The IT List may be responsible for breaking my face, but it was also bonding me and my sister together!

"Of course I can keep a secret!"

Her eyes narrowed.

"Are you sure you won't blab? You don't have a good track record."

She still hadn't forgotten when she was sixteen and I was six and she brought a cute boy over to our house and I marched right up to the cute boy and said, "Hey! You're not the same boy my sister was kissing yesterday, are you?" And it was superawkward because this was their first date. And their last.

"I promise I won't blab!" I held up my hand, like Scout's honor, though, considering my cookie-stealing dismissal from Troop 10, that wasn't the best gesture for boosting my sister's confidence in me.

"Okay," she said, looking around the room as if my parents were inside the pantry eavesdropping. "I'm waiting for a letter from school. An important letter."

"But Mom and Dad don't open your mail...."

"This important letter won't be addressed to me. It will

be addressed to them. But it's about me. And I'd rather tell them the contents of that letter myself."

"Oh!" I burst out. "Is it, like, an award?"

And then my sister's whole face lit up like a Ferris wheel at night.

"Yes!" She hugged me again as if I were the one winning the award. "That's exactly it! And I want to tell them about it personally. So it's more meaningful."

"Like you coming here to tell me about making the CHEER TEAM!!!"

I said this even though I knew that wasn't her original reason for driving over here.

"Yes," my sister said. "Like that." Then she snapped her fingers and said, "Oh! Sherri—I mean, Miss Garcia—wants you to call her. That's how special you are!"

I must say, I still had serious doubts that I'd made the squad. I figured Miss Garcia just wanted to make sure I was still alive and my parents wouldn't sue the school. But until I knew for sure, I decided the best thing would be to keep the details of my disastrous tryout to myself.

"So...how's the rest of the IT List going?" Bethany asked as she opened a cabinet, removed a box of granola bars, and stuffed it into her large handbag.

"Well, you know I was so focused on the CHEER TEAM!!! tryouts that..."

"Any hot prospects for number three?"

IT List #3: Pick your first boyfriend wisely. Bethany asked this in the same supergirlie tone my mom uses whenever she asks if there's a *special someone* in my life.

"Uh... well..." I stammered.

"Come on, Jess! Don't hold out on me!"

Why did everyone assume I was harboring a secret crush on someone? Why was it so impossible to believe that I just wasn't interested in boys that way? Especially when the only time any boys paid attention to me at all was to copy my Pre-Algebra homework?

The only exception was Woodshop. As The Only Girl in the Room, the rest of the class had come to see me as a representative of all femalekind.

"Are girls ever into guys who are shorter than they are?" asked Squiggy.

"When do girls fart?" asked Mouth.

"Why are girls always saying they want nice guys, but then they go for jerks?" asked Cheddar.

"Seriously. Girls fart, right? Why don't they ever just let one rip?" asked Mouth.

They asked these questions because there was nothing at stake. None of them would ever see me as dating material. And vice versa. The only one who never asked me any questions was Aleck. Aleck never said anything to me at all.

Anyway, I could tell from the look of anticipation on my sister's face that this answer wouldn't cut it. With a silent apology to Bridget, I lied.

"I think I might like this boy named Burke Roy? He's cute and popular and a football player?"

Despite my lackluster delivery, this was exactly the sort of thing my sister wanted to hear.

"It sounds like you've picked a winner!" Bethany said, taking a six-pack of flavored seltzer out of the refrigerator and handing it to me. "And you'll have no problem getting him now that you're on the CHEER TEAM!!!"

I really, really found it hard to believe that I was actually on the CHEER TEAM!!! The reality of me being on the CHEER TEAM!!! seemed as likely as the reality of a boy like Burke Roy asking out a girl like me. Not that I even *wanted* to be asked out by him or anyone, which is what led to this stupid fib in the first place.

As I carried the seltzer out to her car for her, Bethany and I worked it out so I'd keep an eye on the mail so she wouldn't have to do so much driving and sneaking around.

"Check every day, but the college almost always mails out these uh…*announcements* on Mondays, so make sure to do an extraspecial check on Tuesdays, okay?"

I'm not sure what "extraspecial" checking would entail, but I promised anyway.

"You're sure you can keep your mouth shut?" she asked once more as she checked her appearance in the rearview mirror.

"I'm not six years old anymore!"

"You're right! You're a young woman! On the CHEER TEAM!!! Call Sherri! I mean, Miss Garcia!"

And then my sister cheerfully *honk-honk-h-honk-honked* the horn and drove off.

At this point, I was pretty much convinced that Miss Garcia was pranking me and Bethany. But I wanted to have the matter settled before I returned to school the next day. I needed to know where I stood. So I called the number Bethany had written down for me on a slip of paper.

Miss Garcia picked up on the first ring.

"Helllllooooo!" She sounded even peppier on the phone than she did in person.

"Uh, hello, Miss Garcia? This is, uh, Jessica Darling. Bethany's sister? She told me that you wanted me to call?"

"Of course!" Miss Garcia replied. "I'm so glad you called! Did she tell you the news! You're on the CHEER TEAM!!!"

Even though I heard her say it, I still couldn't quite believe it.

"Uh, Miss Garcia? You know who I am, right? I'm not

the blonde. I'm the one who...uh...I showed you what I got and I, uh—"

Thankfully she cut me off before I relived my face-first landing.

"I know who you are! And I know who the blonde is, too! She's Bridget Milhokovich! Don't tell her yet because the list won't be posted until tomorrow morning, but she's the new five-foot-four spot in The Famous Pineville Junior High Arrow Pointing Toward Awesomeness Alignment! It's our signature alignment!"

I didn't catch much of what Miss Garcia said after that because I was simultaneously experiencing two opposing emotions:

JOY! My best friend made the CHEER TEAM!!!

JEALOUSY! My best friend made the CHEER TEAM!!! and STOLE MY SPOT.

I only checked back into the conversation when I realized that Miss Garcia had stopped speaking and was waiting for me to answer a question.

"Uh...I'm sorry. What?"

"I know! You're stunned!" she said. "It's such an honor, right? Such an important responsibility! You're overwhelmed! But I wouldn't have offered you this awesome opportunity unless I thought you were up to the task!"

This all sounded very exciting. The only problem was that I had no idea what she was talking about.

"Could you just, uh...repeat the offer?" I said. "I want to be sure I heard you correctly."

"I want you to be the Official Pineville Junior High School Mascot!" she gushed. "Mighty the Seagull!"

Then she went on to say that she had wanted to bring back this time-honored tradition ever since she became head CHEER TEAM!!! coach. But until my death-defying face-plant, she'd never seen a candidate dare to put her personal philosophy in action.

"Cheer without fear!" she chanted.

"Cheer without fear!" I chanted back, because that's the kind of power Miss Garcia has over people.

"You're perfect!" she gushed.

Perfect.

There was that word again.

Plus, I fit the bird suit.

But that wasn't the most important part.

"The identity of Mighty the Seagull must be a mystery! I want the whole school wondering what unique person embodies PJHS pride! Joy! Honor! Spirit!" She lowered her voice to signal the seriousness of what she was about to say. "Can you keep a secret?"

I thought of my promises to Bridget. And Bethany.

"Of course I can," I said. "You can count on me."

Then Miss Garcia told me that I'd be making my debut as Mighty the Seagull at the big pep rally at the end of the week. She encouraged me to study up on what she called "the mascotting arts." I wasn't sure how to do this, but I assured her I would.

"Cheer without fear!" she said once more before hanging up.

So I'm not a cheerleader. But being Mighty the Seagull fulfills IT List #2 because I *am* on the CHEER TEAM!!!

Even if it's on a technicality.

And requires me to wear a giant bird costume.

Anonymously.

Hence the ***asterisks.***

I had barely hung up the phone when it rang again.

It was Bridget, which was surprising because she usually doesn't call. She just shows up uninvited. I assumed she was concerned about the state of my face but was too squeamish to see the damage in person. I was wrong.

"Is there something you want to tell me?" she asked.

Bridget's tone was accusatory in a way that made me nervous because—duh!—there were a whole bunch of things I wanted to tell her but couldn't.

"Uhhhh," I stammered. "What?"

This conversation was going to be harder than I thought.

"I saw your sister at a stop sign when I was walking home from cheer tryouts and..."

She said it in a leading way, like I was supposed to fill in the gap.

"Annnnnd?" I asked back.

There was a moment of silence before Bridget continued.

"And Bethany said something that, I don't know..."

Ack. Why couldn't Bethany keep her mouth shut? Why did she have to brag about me making the CHEER TEAM!!! to Bridget? I swore to Miss Garcia I wouldn't reveal my mascot assignment to anyone. I had to make a choice: either break that promise or lie to my best friend. If all goes the way it should, no one should ever find out that I'm the school mascot. And if Bridget never found out that I was the mascot, she'd never know I lied.

Right?

"Look, Bridget," I said. "I know what Bethany told you, but she's totally wrong. She has no idea what she's talking about."

"She is?" Bridget asked meekly. "She doesn't?"

"When has Bethany ever known more about me than you do?"

RIGHT NOW, I thought guiltily.

"Never," Bridget admitted. "I guess."

I could tell that Bridget was coming around, so I decided to take the conversation in a totally different direction.

"But it *is* true that I've been keeping a secret."

I swear Bridget squeaked like Jazzy the Gerbil when I grabbed him too hard by the tail. I took a deep breath and made my voice sound as serious as possible.

"I stuff my bra."

Silence. Then…laughter. All the laughter she must have kept inside when I landed on my face at tryouts.

"You stuff your bra?" Bridget asked incredulously. "But I thought you had to wear a bra before you could stuff it!"

She had a point there.

"Okay, okay," I said in resignation. "So I stuff my non-supportive training bralette."

When Bridget laughed some more I was encouraged to keep going.

"A cotton ball fills both cups," I added. "And by that I mean a single cotton ball, divided in two. So that's my big confession. Do you feel better now?"

"Yes," Bridget said, still giggling. "And I'm sorry about earlier." I could practically hear her ears turning pink. "You know, the stuff about your sister. She just caught me at a bad time, I guess. I was just, you know, coming down from my tryout freak-out…."

I assured her that no apology was necessary and that everything would work out perfectly.

"And that's a promise!" I said.

These were more than just reassuring words. I already knew them to be true.

Chapter Seventeen

Do you know how hard it is to keep a secret? And I've got more than one!

Fortunately, I was only expected to keep the secret about Bridget making the CHEER TEAM!!! until she found out for herself. As it was, I almost spilled, like, a bazillion times on the bus ride to school! Bridget was in a full-on freak-out, the likes of which I hadn't seen since getting her braces off had boosted her confidence. She was so agitated that she forgot to flirt with Burke Roy and totally ignored him when he flirted with her. For a short while, it was almost like the old Bridget was back.

"Do you think I made the team? I don't know if I made the team! I hope I made the team! I really, really want to make the team! I think I was good enough to make the team, but there were a lot of girls who were good enough to make the team and maybe Miss Garcia liked those girls more than me and—oh! I wish you could have been there to see my tryout because I know you'd be honest about my chances...."

Then she stopped talking, suddenly remembering the embarrassing face-breaking circumstances that led to my early dismissal from the tryout.

"Your face doesn't look nearly as bad as I thought it would," Bridget said brightly.

To her credit, she didn't even try to assure me that I had a shot at making the team. Which was, you know, ironic because I TOTALLY HAD A SPOT ON THE TEAM BUT COULDN'T TELL HER OR ANYONE ELSE ABOUT IT.

The CHEER TEAM!!! list was posted on the bulletin board closest to the front entrance, where everyone in school was guaranteed to see it whether they wanted to or not. Bridget and Dori had promised to meet outside by the flagpole so they could find out together who made the team. They extended their arms, then sandwiched their hands, one atop the other, psyching themselves up to face their fate.

"ONE! TWO! THREE! FOUR!" they chanted. "WALK! THROUGH! THE! DOOR!"

And then they did. I followed.

I already knew Bridget made the CHEER TEAM!!! And yet despite knowing that Dori was a better gymnast than she was, I still held that grape jelliness against her, I guess. So I was shocked when *both* girls jumped up and down with joy.

"I made it! You made it!" Dori squealed.

"WE MADE IT!" Bridget squealed back.

It was a sweet moment and I wish I could have joined in. But I couldn't. I had a secret to keep. So I felt kind of guilty when Bridget and Dori went out of their way to console me for not making the squad.

I made it, too, I wanted to say. *3ZNUF! 4EVA!*

The sweetness was short-lived, however. Manda and Sara's arrival on the scene brought it to a screeching halt. Ha. In more ways than one.

"Omigod! You!" Sara screeched, pointing at Bridget. "And *YOU?*"

That was directed at Dori, obviously. Sara's screeching continued.

"Those were our spots! YOU STOLE OUR SPOTS."

She said this as if the positions on the squad were no different from the table she'd claimed in the cafeteria: hers for the taking. But then I realized that my reaction to Bridget making the team had been exactly the same. It was not my proudest moment.

Bridget and Dori knew better than to stick around for Sara's tirade. They escaped arm in arm as quickly as possible. Meanwhile, Manda kept her hands cupped over her face and mouth and breathed deeply, like in the movies when someone tries to calm down by hyperventilating into a paper bag. Then she turned on her patent leather flats and walked away without saying a word, which was fine because Sara was OMIGOD-ing enough for both of them.

I felt a gentle tap on my shoulder. It was Hope.

"This should be interesting," she said.

"How so?" I asked.

We set off down the hall together, me taking two steps for every one of hers. It's not that Hope is a speed walker or anything, it's just that her legs are, like, twice as long as mine are.

"I've known Manda and Sara forever," Hope said, weaving her way through the crowded hall. "There's no way that they're going to let this go without a fight. They'll definitely seek revenge."

Hope darted left and just barely avoided getting sticked in the face by a pack of chatty field hockey players.

"Revenge? On who? For what?"

"On Bridget and Dori for stealing 'their' spots."

I cautiously sidestepped a kissing eighth-grade couple. What would make them do this right in the middle of the hall in front of everyone? Were they overwhelmed by the romantic atmosphere created by the trash cans and recycling bins?

"But they were dismissed from tryouts for being late," I said. "It was their own fault!"

"They don't see it that way. They see this as a wrong that was done to them. A wrong that needs to be righted. Right now. I guarantee they're putting together a plan."

"What do you think they'll do?" I asked.

"That's the only part I can't predict." She stopped and smiled slyly. "I don't have a devious mind."

Then Hope waved good-bye and continued down the hall, a full head and shoulders above everyone else in the crowd. I admired how she didn't slouch or try to hide her height in any way. Hope wore her differences proudly while I didn't even have the nerve to wear my sister's "interesting" vintage T-shirts.

Anyway, Sara was conspicuously absent from homeroom. "Girl stuff" excuse again, I'm sure. I knew Hope was right. I bet I could find Sara in the girls' bathroom with Manda. Planning. Plotting. Scheming.

But I didn't go looking for them. I stayed put in my seat because I didn't want to get any more involved than I already was. And first period would come soon enough anyway.

Scheme or no scheme, I figured there was no way they'd calm down before Language Arts. I was sure that they'd trick Miss Orden into thinking their psycho rants against "the suckiness of cheerleaders and the idiots who worship them" were actually about the Socs versus the Greasers in *The Outsiders* even though our class had already moved on to *To Kill a Mockingbird*.

But they didn't make any rants. They didn't even make any ranty faces.

There was just the petition.

"Omigod! Hope! Jess! You have to sign the petition."

Now when I heard Sara say "the petition" I assumed that she was asking for the signatures of all Pineville Junior High students who wanted Bridget and Dori kicked off the CHEER TEAM!!! so she and Manda could have those spots—SPOTS STOLEN FROM THEM—instead.

But it wasn't that kind of petition at all.

"The Pineville Junior High Spirit Squad?" I asked.

Hope arched an eyebrow but said nothing.

"It's a new club we're starting," Manda said casually. "We need a minimum of twenty-five signatures from interested students included in our application. We already got twelve names and first period just started."

I was...surprised. And sort of impressed, to tell you

the truth. Manda and Sara had turned anger into action in under fifteen minutes.

Hope looked at the paper on the clipboard.

"The Pineville Junior High Spirit Squad," Hope read aloud. "An all-new, elite, invitation-only organization of…"

She stopped reading, bit her lip, and shoved the petition in my face for me to finish.

"An all-new, elite, invitation-only organization of…" I stopped, then struggled to get the last two words out, to succeed where Hope had failed. "…of…"

"ATHLETIC SUPPORTERS!" Hope yelped.

Okay. Manda and Sara should have put a little bit more thought into the petition before moving forward.

Athletic supporters?

We died laughing.

"BWAHAHAHAHAHAHAHAHA!"

Seriously, we died. And we died again when Manda and Sara totally couldn't understand what we were laughing at or why. They didn't take too kindly to this and threatened to ban us from their club that didn't even exist yet.

"Go ahead and laugh, you two," Manda said. "Just because you don't have what it takes to be an athletic supporter…"

Seriously. How many times could a person die of laughter in one day?

"Maybe you're right. Maybe I don't have what it takes to be"—I tried so hard to keep a straight face—"an athletic supporter."

"I am not the stuff," Hope said, trying equally as hard, "an athletic supporter is made of...."

I swear we would have kept this up all day if Scotty Glazer, G&T's top athlete, hadn't told Manda that "athletic supporters" are more commonly known as "jockstraps."

"The thing we wear under our uniforms to protect our"—he paused—"*you know.*"

"Ew!" Manda said.

"OMIGOD!" Sara said.

And Hope and I died laughing all over again, which really did not make Manda and Sara happy at all. So we made it up to them by signing the petition even though neither one of us had any intention of actually joining this club.

"I kind of hate sports," Hope whispered conspiratorially.

"Me too!" I confessed.

"If we're lucky," Hope said, watching Manda and Sara flit around the room for more signatures, "they'll stay mad enough, long enough, and decide we're not worthy of an invitation anyway."

Before today Hope had never spoken so openly about

how…well…*different* she was from Manda and Sara. I was curious.

"How did you all become friends?" I asked.

"Manda lives on my block," she said with a shrug. "Sara's family used to live close by, too. Until her parents made all that Boardwalk money and moved to a *fancy* house."

She used a funny fake accent for the word *fancy*. Hope was funny. Really funny. I appreciated her sense of humor.

Anyway, after a slight editing of the mission statement that changed "athletic supporters" to "sports lovers," Manda and Sara had no problem getting more than enough signatures for their new club. They were already getting drunk on their power. They loved the idea of being the ones to decide who was cool and who was uncool. Who was in and who was out. The crazy thing is, the more exclusive they made the Spirit Squad sound to potential members, the more potential members were willing to sign.

By the time eighth period rolled around, Manda was vowing to "end the CHEER TEAM!!! monopoly on school spirit and take them down once and for all."

Because nothing says school spirit like declaring war on your fellow classmates.

So I was really dreading the inevitable scene when Bridget joined us at lunch. But that's because I wasn't giving

Bridget enough credit to handle her own business. She had figured out how to deal with the situation for herself.

"Would you be, like, mad at me if I sat with Dori during lunch?" She had caught me in the hall just outside the cafeteria doors. Her ears were bright red. "Not, like, every day! Just some days. Um, today."

I thought it was great that Bridget and Dori had rekindled their friendship. 3ZNUF! 4EVA! And yet I couldn't help but wonder why she hadn't invited me to join them. Before long, Bridget answered my unasked question.

"You can totally join us if you want to, but we'll probably be doing a lot of CHEER TEAM!!! talk and... well..."

And as far as she knew I had tried out for the CHEER TEAM!!! and gotten nothing but an accidental nose job for my troubles. She had no idea that I was on the team, too.

"It's fine," I said. "I understand. *Go.*"

It maybe came out more sharply than I had intended. Bridget took a few steps toward Dori's table, then stopped.

"Are you sure?"

And I said I was totally, totally sure even though I wasn't. I don't know what I was feeling at that moment exactly.

In between.

I didn't say much back at the round table. I could sense Hope trying to catch my attention whenever Manda or

Sara made a snide remark about Bridget sitting at the Not table with Dori...but I concentrated on my lunch instead. This was hard to do because I'd lost my appetite.

Is this the IT clique I'm supposed to stick with?

I'd ask Bethany, but I already knew what her answer would be.

Chapter Eighteen

I worked so hard. So so so hard. Honestly, I've never focused on homework like that in my life! Not in Language Arts, Español, or any of the other usual subjects.

This was *mascot* homework.

All week I studied professional mascots during whatever games my dad had on TV. I watched Bridget practice her cheers at the bus stop in the morning. I mimicked moves from videos of Bethany's squad back in the day. This morning I chugged a gallon of performance-enhancing energy drink with extra vitamins, minerals, and caffeine.

THE PEP RALLY WAS TODAY. AND I WAS READY.

Putting my time and energy into pep rally prep had taken my mind off just about everything else going on. Like what? Oh, you know, like failing Woodshop, not having a clue how to pick my first boyfriend wisely, worrying that my fractured group of friends didn't qualify as an IT clique, and so on. I think that's what a hobby is supposed to do for you. It helps you stop thinking about things. Of course, this only works when your hobby *isn't* thinking about things.

Anyway, Miss Garcia had slipped me the key to the CHEER TEAM!!! changing room with instructions to get there right at the start of sixth period. She knew it would be empty because all the cheerleaders had worn their uniforms to school. She forbade me from seeing the bird suit until minutes before the pep rally began. She said it was because she didn't want anyone to see me in the bird suit and spoil the secret. I did as I was told and arrived right at the final bell—on schedule but without much time to get ready. I didn't hesitate to unzip one of two PJHS garment bags I knew had to be for me.

ZZZZZZZIP! WHOOSH! ACHOOOOOO!

Red, white, and blue feathers flew out of the bag as if they were still attached to real live birds. I sucked half a flock up my nose, which immediately and inevitably triggered the sneezing attack to end all sneezing attacks.

And this was just the first bag.

With a runny nose and watery eyes, I struggled to open the second bag. It was more gruesome than the first—like a cross between a backstage visit to *The Muppet Show* and a butcher's shop. There was a bulgy-eyed, squeaky-beaked bird head; a set of fluffy slippers shaped like talons; and a pair of wings designed to slide over my arms like the most over-the-top prom gloves ever.

There was no time to waste. The pep rally was already underway.

"Cheer without fear," I told myself. "Cheer without fear."

It took me about ten minutes and ten thousand sneezes to put the whole costume on. The whole time, I could hear Miss Garcia's voice leading cheers on the loud-speakers.

"A-W-E" *[clap clap]* "S-O-M-E!" *[stomp stomp]*

When I turned to try to look at myself in the full-length mirror, my tail feathers brushed across a shelf and sent a decade's worth of Pineville Junior High CHEER TEAM!!! trophies clattering to the floor.

Whoops.

But I didn't have time to clean up my mess. I didn't have any time to get used to my own body. I heard Miss Garcia's voice calling my name over the speakers.

"Mighty the Seagull! Where are yooooooooou?"

It was now or never. Honestly, I would have chosen never. But that wasn't an option. Where could I escape to wearing a red-white-and-blue-feathered bird suit that weighed more than I did?

"Mighty the Seagull! Where are yooooooooou?"

I channeled the team spirit of the Phillie Phanatic, the San Diego Chicken, and other great mascots that had come before me. I ran out to center court and opened my wings wide to the crowd as if to say, "Here I am, world! The mascot you've been waiting for!"

I made it about five steps before tripping on my talons and falling beak over tail feather. Fortunately, feathers are excellent for shock absorption. Not only was I unhurt, I seemed to bounce off the ground and land right back on my feet. It's like I had totally meant to fall down and the gales of laughter from the audience were exactly what I'd intended.

I didn't even have to consider whether I should try to fall again. It came all too naturally to me in these oversized claws. But, as before, I rebounded so quickly that I was able to do a sort of full-feathered equivalent of jazz hands when I got back up.

"TA-DA!"

I couldn't really get a good look at the crowd, but I could hear them. And judging by their boisterous cheers and applause, the audience loved me. And they loved me even more when I heard music play the opening notes of the Pineville Junior High Fight Song! The choreography for this routine was a tradition and hadn't changed since Bethany's days on the squad. From watching her old videos, I knew every hip wiggle, every shimmy, every shake-shake-shake.

I did them all.

Once I'd gotten used to it, I was somehow more graceful in the bird suit than I was out of it. And it was after my perfectly executed stop-drop-booty-pop that I heard the first person in the crowd ask the question.

"Who are you?"

Others joined in.

"Who are you? Who are you?"

It gained momentum quickly.

"Whooooooooooo are yoooooou?" the crowd roared. "Whooooo are yoooooou?"

Weird, right? That's what Mr. Pudel had sung at me on my first day of school! I couldn't help but wonder if my Woodshop teacher had somehow put the crowd up to this chant. But I quickly dismissed the idea because Mr. Pudel had no clue that I was the student inside the suit. It was just a coincidence.

"Whooooooo are yoooooou?"

A freaky coincidence.

And yet, the louder they chanted, the more I was

tempted to say good-bye to anonymity. Why not remove the bird head and show the whole school that I, Jessica Darling, was the seventh-grade mastermind behind the most brilliant display of school mascotting since the invention of fake feathers? Miss Garcia would surely understand my quest for glory! I had just about settled on the idea when I discovered there was one major problem with this plan.

The bird head was stuck.

Like, really, really stuck. I don't know if the feathers were caught in the zipper or what. All I knew was that I was trapped inside this bird head and the air quality inside the beak was already very poor and certainly wasn't going to get better if I started up a full-fledged fit of a FREAK-OUT.

Which is exactly what I did.

"Whoooooo are yoooooou? Whoooooo are yoooooou?"

I flapped my wings wildly to get the attention of the CHEER TEAM!!!, but they just played to the crowd, like, "Omigod! Isn't our mascot hilarious? Aren't we all so totally hot?"

There's no doubt that I was actually—not metaphorically—the hottest person in that gym. It had to be a bazillion degrees inside that bird suit and getting hotter by the millisecond. I used up what precious oxygen

I had by calling to Bridget for help, but it came out sounding like this.

"Helllllllblurgh!"

No joke. I was having a total hyperventilating panic attack. Desperate, I started ramming my bird head into the cheerleaders' faces, hoping to get their attention. I succeeded only in causing the collapse of the famous Pineville Junior High Pyramid of Perfection. Screaming cheerleaders toppled to the floor like bowling pins in a strike.

How the audience reacted to this, I honestly have no idea. I couldn't see or hear anything but my own blood boiling inside my eardrums and eyeballs. My survival instincts had kicked in and I was only concerned about self-preservation. With what remaining strength I had, I headed straight for the bleachers. There were hundreds of students and teachers in the audience. Surely one of them would rescue me! I tugged wildly at the bird head and yelled "Helllllllblurgh!" to anyone who would listen. But everyone was too busy laughing and hooting to hear me.

"Whoooooooooo are yoooooooooou? Whoooooooooo are yooooooou?"

It was at that moment that I accepted my fate. This seagull was dead meat.

And with my last raggedy breaths I asked myself, "Whoooooooooo am I? Whoooooooooo am IIIIIIII?"

Yes, I decided to die with dignity. Or as much dignity as one can have when wearing a giant bird suit. I planted my fluffy talons on the first row of bleacher seats, saluted the crowd, then did a perfect swan dive—or, uh, seagull dive—right onto the CHEER TEAM!!! practice mat.

Only I didn't land on the mat. I was caught...by Miss Garcia!

The crowd roared louder than ever as Miss Garcia dragged me by my wings all across the gym floor, through the locker room, and into the changing room.

I could still hear them cheering, even behind the closed door.

She locked the door and pulled the blinds closed before unhooking my bird head. She didn't want to take any chances of spoiling my secret identity.

"Do you hear that? They love you! I knew you were the right person for the job! I loved the dramatic improvisation!"

I was still sort of dizzy from lack of oxygen so it was difficult for me to muster any enthusiasm besides a thumbs—or rather, wing—up.

Miss Garcia reminded me of my "cover story" before I changed back into my regular jeans and T-shirt for seventh period. I had very little time to compose myself before facing my friends in the cafeteria.

"Omigod! Jess! Where were you? You missed the craziness!"

"What craziness?" I asked innocently, swatting an imaginary feather off my shoulder.

"The pep rally!" Sara explained. "It was insane! Where were you?"

I knew Sara would keep asking unless I said something. Fortunately, Miss Garcia had prepared me.

"I was at the nurse's office," I said. "Girl stuff."

And then I clutched my abdomen like I'd seen the other girls do when they had "girl stuff." It must have worked because Manda made a face.

"Ew. Say no more."

"So you missed the whole thing?" Sara pressed. "With the crazy chicken?"

"Seagull," Hope corrected under her breath but loud enough for me to hear.

"What crazy chicken?" I asked, playing dumb.

And that's when Bridget and Dori showed up and went off.

"THE CRAZY CHICKEN THAT STOLE ALL THE ATTENTION AWAY FROM US."

I've known Bridget for twelve years and I can honestly say I've never seen her so mad. Not even when I gave her favorite Colonial-era American Girl doll a punk makeover. Manda and Sara were unmoved.

"Omigod! Boo hoo hoo!" And then Sara wiped away fake tears.

"We worked really hard on our routine and all anyone can talk about is that crazy chicken!" Bridget griped.

I noticed that Hope couldn't stop herself from mouthing, "Seagull."

Then Dori was emboldened to speak up.

"We were so mondo and no one noticed!"

Manda gave her the side eye.

"First of all, puh-leeze," she said. "No one says *mondo* anymore."

Sara did a double take. This was news to her. But she played along.

"Omigod! Everyone knows that."

"Second of all," Manda continued, "you're obviously just jealous."

This was a bold statement to be made by someone who was so jealous that she'd started a spirit war.

"Personally, I loved the mascot," Manda went on.

"Omigod! Me too!" Sara added.

"I think the chicken showed a lot of school spirit!"

I swear Hope almost choked on her potato chips.

And so none of my closest friends suspected that I was the mascot the whole school was buzzing about. I was the most popular and most anonymous person at Pineville

Junior High. As I headed to last period, it was so weird to overhear eighth graders talking about me, having no idea that it was me they were talking about.

"Burke Roy is the chicken."

"Dude, he's on the football team. He's not the chicken."

"Burke's *hi*-larious. It's got to be him."

"He was right there in the gym wearing his football uniform. It's not Burke."

"*BurkeBurkeBurke*. You know. Like a chicken."

"Duh."

"Whozit then?"

"I don't know. But whoever the chicken is, he's *hi*-larious."

"Why's our mascot a chicken, anyway?"

I thought of Hope. I came this close to shouting "Seagull!" But I didn't.

It's interesting that almost everyone assumed Mighty was a boy. That only a boy could possibly act so daring and uninhibited, that no girl could take herself so unseriously and risk making a *hi*-larious fool out of herself in front of the whole school....

I started getting mad about it. Why assume that all girls will act helpless and timid and—ugh—*girlie-girlie* when put in a stereotypical "boy" situa—

Oh. Ohhhhhh.

Hadn't I been acting all helpless and timid and—ugh—girlie-girlie in Woodshop?

I had.

But no more. Not today! No! Today I had cheered without fear! Now I would woodshop without fear! I would make my spoon if it killed me! Though it would be much better if it didn't kill me, right? I'd like to survive long enough to use it on a pint of cookie dough ice cream.

I was pretty psyched up when I got to eighth period. All week long, while all the boys had been making their spoons, and asking me about girls and farts and girls' farts, I had done nothing but study the spoon-making instructions. I had all the steps memorized by now. I knew what to do.

I just had to do it.

"Woodshop without fear," I said to myself as I selected a block of soft maple.

"Woodshop without fear," I repeated as I traced the spoon template.

"Woodshop without fear," I said once more as I turned the handle of the vise to get a better grip on the woodblock.

I'd been so focused on my task that I hadn't paid the slightest bit of attention to anything else going on around me. Until Mr. Pudel made it impossible not to.

"WHAT IS THIS?"

Mr. Pudel was hovering over someone I couldn't see. And yet, I knew that someone was Aleck. And I was right.

"It's my project," I heard Aleck's voice say.

"THAT'S NOT A SPOON."

"Thank you for noticing," Aleck said, seemingly unintimidated. "It's not a spoon. It's a toothpick."

"A toothpick." Mr. Pudel said it in a way that expressed both disbelief and *no duh*.

"An *epic* toothpick! See? I personalized it!"

From where I stood, this "epic" toothpick looked no different from a regular toothpick. But Mr. Pudel held the "epic toothpick" up to the light, turning it this way and that, as if he were appraising its value like an expert on those boring shows my mom loves to watch where people try to make money off the junk in their attics by calling them antiques.

"Does this toothpick say PROPERTY OF MR. PUDEL?"

"*Epic* toothpick," Aleck corrected. "And, yep!"

"How did you even *do* that?" Mr. Pudel sounded genuinely impressed.

I was too busy watching them to notice that I hadn't stopped turning the handle of the vise.

"YOW!"

I totally squashed my index finger! It hurt. A lot. Then in my panic, I spun the handle even tighter in the wrong direction. It hurt even worse.

"YOOOOOWZA!!!"

Within seconds Mr. Pudel rushed over and rescued me from the clutches of the vise. I spun in crazy circles around the room, winging my hands wildly through the air.

"YOW! YOW! YOW!"

I collided into shelves, sending several classes' worth of napkin holders and spoons crashing to the floor.

"YOW! YOW! YOWZA!"

Mr. Pudel caught me by my spinning shoulders and went into ER mode.

"Aleck! Get Clem to the nurse! I don't trust her to make it on her own!"

I was still too busy hooting and flapping in pain to carry a conversation or to be even the least bit nervous about being alone with a boy. A boy who happened to be Aleck. The only boy in class who hadn't bothered to ask me anything. At all. Ever.

It wasn't until we made it all the way to the infirmary on the other side of the school—you'd think it would be closer to Woodshop's hall considering the risk to our lives and limbs—that Aleck spoke. It was the first time he'd ever spoken to me. This is what he said:

"Helllllllblurgh."

I guess my hooting and flapping was reminiscent of the way a certain feathered mascot hooted and flapped around the gym during the pep rally. Before I could squawk in denial, he pressed his finger to his lips and shushed.

"Don't worry, Clem," Aleck assured me as he opened the door to the infirmary. "Your secret is safe with me."

And for some reason, I believed him.

Chapter Nineteen

This is what it's like to have a secret identity.

Correction: *almost*-secret identity, as Aleck likes to remind me in Woodshop every single day. But I'll get to him later. Important people first. Like Bridget.

Bridget hates me. She doesn't know she hates me, but she does.

"Grrrrrr! I hate our mascot!" she complained on the walk to the bus stop. "Dori and I just don't understand why Miss Garcia lets that chicken cheapen the art of cheer!"

"Seagull…"

"WHATEVER. I HATE THAT UGLY CHICKEN WITH A PASSION."

Three things struck me about this statement:

1. Bridget had never hated anything before.

2. Was I really ugly? Gaudy maybe. But ugly?

3. WHY DID EVERYONE THINK I WAS A CHICKEN?

Anyway, I'd thought it was bad when Bridget went to CHEER TEAM!!! practice after school and I had to ride the bus home alone every day. I thought it was worse when Bridget started sitting with the CHEER TEAM!!! at lunch on Fridays. And I thought it was way, *way* worse when she joined Dori at the square table near the kitchen at least twice a week besides that.

But this—being the UGLY BIRD my best friend HATED WITH A PASSION—was the worst of all.

I can't say I didn't see this rift between me and Bridget coming. I mean, I knew there would be consequences for Bridget's prettiness. But I didn't think it would happen like this. I assumed that it would go the usual way. You know, she'd get a boyfriend and forget all about me. And if the flirting she does with Burke Roy is any indication, it will *still* happen that way. It just hasn't happened yet.

I should look to Bridget for flirty inspiration because I'm supposed to move on to IT List #3: Pick your first boyfriend wisely. But I'm way more clueless about boys than I ever was about clothes or the CHEER TEAM!!!, which is really saying something because I *still* know NEXT TO NOTHING about either one of those subjects.

The only boy in school who seems to know I exist is

Aleck, but he doesn't count. I've noticed him messing around in the halls in between classes and it seems to me that annoying girls is his hobby. Actually, now that I think about it, I don't know if he's trying to be annoying. I mean, Aleck doesn't act all that different from Burke Roy. Only when Burke Roy shoves a baseball cap over girls' eyes or pulls on girls' ponytails or snaps girls' bra straps, the girls generally—and Bridget specifically—get all googly-eyed and giggly. When Aleck does those same exact things, they just get annoyed.

I don't know whether he's trying to annoy girls or if he's just naturally gifted at the art of annoyance. Whatever the reason, for the first few weeks of school I guess Aleck didn't notice there was a girl in Woodshop—me!—he could annoy. I mean, before he guessed my secret identity, he never talked to me at all. Now he talks to me all the time! Let's put it this way: If I put the same energy into passing Woodshop as he did in annoying me during Woodshop, I could have hand-carved a yacht out of a redwood by now.

"Clementine, that is the ugliest piece of flatware I've ever seen," he said, pointing to my lumpy, crooked spoon.

It was true. The spoon was ugly. It was the first C minus I'd ever gotten. A C minus in any of my other subjects would've been a major academic tragedy. But I've never been so proud of such a mediocre grade. I *earned* that C minus! Besides, Mr. Pudel said that with my perfect scores on all the written tests and the improvement I'm already showing on my second project—a napkin holder—I shouldn't worry too much about his class bringing down my whole grade point average.

Aleck started playing percussion with my ugly spoon and a less ugly spoon made by one of his friends. It suddenly dawned on me that he was *waiting.* He had started a conversation and it was now up to me to continue it.

"Um, so what happened with your epic toothpick?" I asked.

"Oh, *that,*" Aleck said. "Mr. Pudel gave me an F plus."

I wasn't sure I heard him correctly over the buzz of the saws.

"An F plus?"

"The first one he's ever given," Aleck said, looking positively psyched.

A shadow cast over us. There was only one man who could make that kind of shade.

"LISTEN UP," Mr. Pudel bellowed.

As if Aleck and I had a choice in the matter.

"Just because you *can* do something doesn't mean you *should,*" he said. "And just because you *can't* do something doesn't mean you *shouldn't.*"

Our teacher walked away and Aleck said, "That was deep."

Then Aleck stopped drumming and deliberately balanced one spoon on the top of his head. His hair was crazier than ever, and the utensil got lost in it.

"Maybe you should use that spoon to comb your hair," I said. "You might actually see some improvement."

Aleck stared at me, stone-faced. Oh no! I'd hurt his feelings....

Then he opened his mouth, tipped back his head, and laughed. A loud HA! HA! HA! kind of laugh. The spoon didn't move.

"You're funny, Clem," Aleck said when he finally settled down. Then he took my ugly spoon and very deliberately balanced it on *my* head, which was much harder to do without the benefit of curls to get lost in.

He looked at me very seriously, which was funny because we both had spoons on our heads. Aleck's eyes are brown, but not a boring brown like mine. They're...I don't know... interesting. I was trying to figure out the difference between his kind of brown eyes and mine when he spoke up.

"I'm a failure."

And even though it was sort of true, I wanted to tell him that he was wrong. But before I could say anything, he hopped on top of his stool.

"With flair!"

Then Aleck jumped off. He landed lightly on his feet, but the spoon slipped and hit the floor with a clunk.

I laughed, but I tried not to laugh too hard because I was determined to keep my ugly spoon balanced on my head. Aleck and I didn't speak the rest of the class period. We worked on our napkin holders. When the dismissal bell rang, I victoriously removed the spoon from where Aleck had placed it forty minutes earlier. I made a point to prod him with it as we herded out the door.

"I win!" I said.

And I really felt like I had won something. Though what it was, I still couldn't tell you.

"You won," Aleck replied. "*This* time."

And I smiled in spite of myself, happy to hear the hint of a *next* time.

Maybe *too* happy.

I was at my locker, idly spinning the combination but without much success. If I didn't hurry up, I'd miss the bus home. But that didn't seem important at the time.

"EARTH TO JESSICA!"

I jolted to attention.

Bridget was suddenly in front of me, though I hadn't taken any notice of where she'd come from or when. Dori was standing right behind her, as she usually did these days.

"Uh, sorry," I apologized.

"What's up with you lately?" she asked. "You're acting weird."

"What do you mean?" I asked.

"Like you're keeping something from me." She narrowed her aquamarine eyes. "And don't tell me you're stuffing your bra!"

She got really close to my face. I could smell the bubble gum on her breath.

"I'm just gonna, like, ask you straight out."

She paused and I braced myself for the dreaded question: *You're the mascot, aren't you?*

"Do. You. Like. Him. Or. Not?"

She spoke slowly and deliberately so there was no mistaking what she had asked. And yet, I had no idea what she had just asked. Or why. I was genuinely and totally confused.

"Me? Who? Wha...?"

Bridget glanced at Dori, like she needed assistance. Dori gave her a "go on" nudge.

"You know who."

Did I? Was Bridget talking about me and...?

Aleck?

Wait! There was no "me and Aleck." How could Bridget know about something that wasn't even a thing?

"I don't know who or what you're talking about," I said.

Bridget flinched but recovered quickly. Her mouth loosened up into something that sort of resembled a smile. I couldn't help but think, *When in doubt, Jess, just smile, smile, smile!*

"Okay," Bridget said. "I guess I believe you."

I knew she didn't believe me. And she knew I knew she didn't believe me because best friends know these things about each other.

But that knowingness didn't make either of us feel any better as we took off in opposite directions down the hall.

Chapter Twenty

That afternoon was Mighty the Seagull's debut at a real game.

My beginning.

My end.

And maybe a new beginning.

But I'm getting ahead of myself.

So things were really, really awkward with Bridget. These days we only saw each other on the bus in the morning, and even then she spent more time flirting with Burke than talking to me. I didn't blame Bridget for being annoyed with me. She knew I was keeping a secret—she just didn't know what it was. And because I couldn't stand the tension between us anymore, I'd decided to tell her the truth about my secret identity after the game. I knew this

would upset Miss Garcia, but she wasn't nearly as important to me as my best friend.

Make that *ex*–best friend.

But I'm getting ahead of myself again.

Despite the nonstop gossip and speculation, no one else
had figured out that I was the one inside the bird suit. And
the one person who did know the truth about my identity
had unexpectedly kept that information to himself.

Sort of.

Right at the end of eighth period today, Aleck went out
of his way to give me a wooden token the size of a quarter.

"For luck," he said before rushing out the door with his
buddies.

He had used the woodworking iron to draw a picture
of Mighty the Seagull on one side and CHEER WITHOUT
FEAR on the other.

How did Aleck even know that was my motto?

But I didn't have time to wonder about Aleck or what
he knew about me. I had to get my game face on. Literally.
You know, the bird head.

It was our football team's opening game against the
Baygate Bears. (Apparently they are our rivals and we're
supposed to hate them because…uh…why?) Bridget and
Dori were making their halftime debut as new members
of the Pineville Junior High CHEER TEAM!!! And if that

weren't enough, it was also the first public appearance by the Pineville Junior High Spirit Squad: Manda and Sara and the select few seventh-grade girls who they had decided were *almost* as cool as they were. All eight girls wore snug SPIRIT SQUAD tees and waved SPIRIT SQUAD signs and whistled and WHOOOOOOED and generally called a lot of attention to themselves.

So anyway. The game was a big deal. It was a gorgeous afternoon for football, even if you weren't really into football. The sun was shining, but the air was cool and crisp and made me want to put on a sweater and snuggle up to share a Styrofoam cup of cocoa with…uh…*someone.* The bleachers were packed with students, teachers, and parents who apparently felt the same way.

Surprisingly, I wasn't nervous about appearing in front of such a huge crowd. I was more concerned with how Bridget would react to the news that I was the ugly bird she hated more than anything else in the world. Besides, whatever I did on the field that afternoon was sure to be way less embarrassing than my death throes at the pep rally. Okay. Maybe I was a teensy bit worried that I'd let down my fans. I mean, there was no way Mighty the Seagull could possibly outdo that first performance, right?

Wrong. Oh so wrong.

It started out just fine, I guess. True, I had hardly taken

ten steps onto the field before I got tangled up in my talons and tripped and did a sort of accidental somersault. (Somer*fault*?) But somehow, someway, I landed right back on my feet.

TA-DA!

There's no way I could've pulled that off if I'd attempted it on purpose.

Then I danced along with Bridget and Dori and the rest of the CHEER TEAM!!! to the official Pineville Junior High Fight Song.

Go, go, go!
Mighty Seagulls!
Fight, fight, fight!
Mighty Seagulls!
Win, win, win!
Mighty Seagulls!

Now those of you unfamiliar with the rat-with-wings better known as the Jersey Shore seagull might think that this is probably the wimpiest school mascot ever. But the Jersey Shore seagulls brought up on the mean streets of the Seaside Heights boardwalk are not to be messed with. They are tough. They will make a beak-sneak-attack on that freshly purchased hot pretzel you just raised to your mouth. They will swoop in and tear that Italian sausage sub sandwich right out of your grubby hands. Seagulls will literally steal cotton candy from a baby.

Seagulls don't play. For real.

But I wasn't feeling mighty at that moment. My silly dancing and comic mugging for the audience was all very uninspired. The fans in the bleachers were bored, and I was probably about two seconds away from getting booed off the field.

Until I felt a tug on my tail feathers.

I craned my bird head around as best as I could to see what was happening.

"HOOOOOONK!"

It was the biggest goose I had ever seen. And he was honking at me.

Why was this bird the only living creature that didn't mistake me for an ugly chicken? Nope, it mistook me for a gorgeous goose.

I don't know if I was pumped up by the pep band, the spirit of competition, or the three liters of Coke I drank before the game, but I instinctively flapped my wings and scared it away. The audience liked this. So I started playing up my victory over the goose by striking bodybuilder poses. The mighty Pineville Junior High seagull had vanquished another foe!

I was still showing off and flexing my bird muscles when I felt a more aggressive nip in my feathered nether regions.

Okaaaaay.

In elementary school, we had a special assembly when a policewoman came in to warn us all about Stranger Danger. She talked about how you just have to trust your gut when it tries to warn you there's something that just isn't right about a certain individual, even if you can't quite put your finger on it. She called it the uh-oh feeling, and when you get the uh-oh feeling you're supposed to forget whatever else you're doing and get the heck away from the source of the sketchiness as soon as possible.

The goose gave me the uh-oh feeling.

He must have interpreted my dancing as some sort of mating display. I wasn't sure if he was intimidated or impressed by my moves and I definitely didn't want to find out. So I panicked. Again.

I took off running with very little idea of where I was even going because the sun was right in my eyes and it's very hard to navigate when you're wearing a giant bird head unless you're an actual giant bird. Like the goose.

He had no problem keeping up with me. He attacked from all directions at once. Feathers—mostly synthetic, mostly mine—flew all over the place. Again, I cried out for help. "Helllllblurgh" must translate to "hey, baby baby" in goose-speak because the goose honked back at me like he was more determined than ever to make me his girl-friend. And this is when I must have really lost my mind because there was a brief moment when I actually wondered if this would qualify as IT List #3: Pick your first boyfriend wisely.

This is also when I must have sprinted past the sidelines and onto the football field right in the middle of a crucial fourth-down play on the third yard line, or so Miss Garcia told me after the fact because I had zero awareness of any-thing that was happening beyond the major panic attack happening inside my bird head.

Suddenly, miraculously, I spotted a flash of activity across the green. I couldn't see very well, but it was huge, brown, and headed right for me. I'd find out later that the opposition's mascot, the Baygate Bear, took my disruption of the game personally. I wasn't trying to sabotage the vis-iting team! I was just trying to get away from the goose! But the Baygate Bear didn't care. It had a score to settle! It came charging after me from the opposite side of the field.

So now I was being attacked by a lovesick goose and a crazed grizzly.

I have no idea how long this chase went on. During a crisis, time simultaneously speeds up and stands still, a description that I know doesn't make any sense, but does anything about this story make sense? Just about the only thing about this story that *does* make perfect sense is what happened next.

I smashed beak-first into the goalpost.

Chapter Twenty-One

When I woke up, I wasn't dead. I was in the nurse's office. But from the murderous look on Bridget's face, I might as well have been dead already.

"YOU!" she yelled. "It was YOU! The whole time!"

There was no denying this. Someone had used the jaws of life to remove the bird head, but from the neck down, I was still Mighty the Seagull. I had lost most of my feathers in the chase so I looked like the scrawniest piece of poultry Bob Cratchit could buy with Scrooge's half a hay penny. My pathetic appearance did not inspire pity from my best friend.

Ex–best friend.

"How could you do this?" she raged. "How could you sabotage everything so important to me! I'm your best friend!"

I tried to explain. "I wasn't trying to—"

She cut me off. I'd never seen Bridget like this before. Fury distorted her face in a very...um...unpretty way I hadn't thought possible.

"You were jealous that I made the team! You're no better than Manda and Sara and their stupid Spirit Squad!"

I was about to deny her accusation when I realized that there was a hint of truth to what she was saying. I wasn't jealous of her making the CHEER TEAM!!! But I did envy how effortlessly she had adjusted to junior high. Bridget was the living example of my sister's IT List. Not me.

And if I was being totally honest, I was a bit jealous of Bridget's rekindled friendship with Dori. What if it turns out 2ZNUF after all?

All these thoughts were zooming around my goal-posted brain. So when I finally got around to arranging them into something I could say that would make sense, it was already too late. Bridget had put up with enough.

"You know, when your sister told me that you had a crush on Burke Roy, I didn't want to believe her...."

WHEN MY SISTER TOLD HER WHAT???

"I was, like, no way. Bethany had no idea what she was talking about! But then you were acting all shady and Dori said I should confront you. So I did! And you lied! You were lying the whole time about everything!"

I was so shocked by this accusation that I inhaled one of the few feathers left on the bird suit.

COUGHCOUGHHACKHACKCHOKECHOKE.

"I don't know who you are anymore," Bridget said, ignoring the fact that I was coughing, hacking, and choking to death. "And I'm not sure I want to."

Bridget exited, and I swear all the air in the room, maybe all the air in the atmosphere, went with her. When I finally yakked up the offending feather, I was too stunned to cry. Was I upset about the false accusations? Or the ones that sort of rang true?

I didn't have time to answer these questions because a few seconds later Nurse Fleet was ushering my parents into the treatment room. I must have been in really bad shape if she was able to persuade both of them to leave whatever they were doing to come get me.

"Are you okay?" Dad and Mom asked simultaneously.

I nodded, though they didn't look convinced. I must have been quite a sorry sight in my goose-pecked, nearly featherless bird suit.

"Her vitals are fine," Nurse Fleet said. "That bird head offers better cranial protection than the football helmets."

Then she shut the door behind her to give us some privacy.

"See? I'm fine," I reassured them in a very unreassuring voice.

Sure, physically, I was fine. But mentally and emotionally, I was a mess. My best friend had just broken up with me!

"You ran into a goalpost?" my mom asked. "Because you're the school mascot?"

"Why didn't you tell us you were the mascot?" my dad asked. "We would've cheered you on."

They weren't asking these questions in a "we are the annoying parents interrogating you" kind of way. They were asking them in a "we need to understand this weirdness" kind of way. And for that, I couldn't blame them. They had no idea that I was living a double life.

"I ran into the goalpost because I *was* the school mascot. And I didn't tell you I was the school mascot because I was supposed to keep my identity secret," I said. "But I don't have to anymore because I'm not the mascot. I'm hanging up my wings."

Talking about it got me all choked up. Not because I was sad to give up the bird suit. I was sad because Bridget had given up on me.

But my parents didn't know that. They looked at each other, then looked at me, speechless. No parenting book has a chapter titled, "What to Say When Your Daughter Dresses Up Like a Deranged Seagull and Almost Cracks Her Skull Open Like an Egg When She Runs Headfirst

Into a Goalpost Because a Goose Wants to Make Her His Girlfriend."

I made it easier for them by giving them something to do. I swallowed my tears and managed to ask for help.

"Speaking of my wings, can you help me get out of this thing?"

While my mom unzipped me out of the bird suit, my dad talked to the nurse just to make sure I was as fine as she said I was. Dad's a noticer. Like me. He knew something wasn't right, but he didn't know what was wrong.

I knew only too well what was wrong.

We were all quiet on the car ride home, which was a relief. I was so afraid that if Mom and Dad asked more questions, I'd just start crying again. And if I started crying again they'd ask more questions about why I was crying and I'd end up telling them about Bridget and how she thought I was lying about not liking Burke Roy when I wasn't lying about that at all, but it was hard to explain because I had lied about Burke Roy to Bethany, which was dumb and I never should have done it, which is why I couldn't even be mad at her for blabbing about it to Bridget since my sister must have figured that if I had a crush on Burke Roy surely Bridget must already know about it because best friends don't keep secrets from each other when, in fact, I had been keeping a secret from Bridget when I didn't reveal my secret identity and even though that wasn't the secret she thought I was keeping, it was almost as bad as the one she thought I was keeping about Burke Roy, which wasn't a secret at all but a lie....

Ack. I can't still straight think.

I still think can't straight.

I STILL CAN'T THINK STRAIGHT.

Maybe the bird head didn't protect my brain after all.

Chapter Twenty-Two

So it's been a week since I permanently retired Mighty the Seagull. Even Miss Garcia agreed that it was the best for everyone involved.

"Tell your sister I'm sorry it didn't work out," she said.

I said I would even though I knew I wouldn't because I wasn't sorry at all.

I was only sorry that Bridget wasn't talking to me. To my surprise, she hadn't told anyone that I was the infamous mascot the whole school was buzzing about. Honestly, I preferred it that way. After all the secret-keeping, I deserved to be the most popular nobody at Pineville Junior High.

Bridget started sitting with Burke on the bus every morning and did an excellent job of pretending I didn't exist. So it wasn't surprising when Sara broke the news to me in homeroom.

"Omigod! I hear Burke is totally going to ask Bridget out, like, officially."

I'd known it was coming, of course. I just wished I'd heard it from Bridget. But I supposed Dori was the friend she confided in now. They sat together at lunch every day. Though being on the CHEER TEAM!!! had boosted their Line Cutting status immensely, they both brought their lunches every day. One day soon they *will* decide to buy and they *will* cut Manda and Sara on line. And that day *will* be a very, very bad day.

I got so deep into my worries that I'd forgotten Sara was talking at me.

"Jess! Is it true?" Sara asked. "You would know, right? You're still Bridget's bestie, right?"

Sara was totally aware that Bridget and I had a falling-out. She was just trying to find out why. Ack. The whole business made me feel sick to my stomach. I raised my hand to get my homeroom teacher's attention.

"I need a pass to the nurse," I groaned. "I think I'm gonna throw up."

When I arrived at the nurse's office, all the cots were empty. It was only homeroom, after all. Barely enough time had passed for any medical emergencies to occur. I clutched my abdomen.

"Girl stuff," I explained.

And this time, it was totally true. It *was* girl stuff that was making me feel so sick. Just not the kind of girl stuff Nurse Fleet typically dealt with. She looked up from her paperwork and her face lit up like she was thrilled to see me. It turned out she *was* thrilled to see me.

"I'm thrilled to see you!" she said.

"You are?"

"I am," she said. "How's your head?"

Such a complicated question. How *was* my head? My head was a mess. But she wasn't referring to the psychological state of my head. She was referring to the physical state of my head, you know, after the goalpost injury. So I answered that question specifically.

"My head is just fine," I said.

"You were amazing out there on the field that day!"

That was not the reaction I was expecting.

"Are you aware that you outran a lovesick goose, a vengeful mascot, and twenty-two football players?"

Uh, let's see. IT WAS ONLY THE TALK OF THE ENTIRE SCHOOL AFTER IT HAPPENED. So yeah, I think I'm aware of that. I bet the whole school would still be talking about it if an anonymous prankster hadn't sent a pair of SpongeBob boxer shorts up the flagpole. Now the whole school was talking about that. Until the next thing happens. See, that's how it is in junior high: Nothing is big news for very long. This is a bummer when it's good news about you worth remembering. But a short attention span is definitely a relief when the news is about you and it's bad.

Nurse Fleet continued.

"I can only imagine what you might be capable of when you aren't weighed down by fifty pounds of feathers!"

By the time I'd run into the goalpost it was more like one pound of feathers, but I didn't have the energy to correct her. And I must have looked totally clueless because that's when Nurse Fleet really started beaming at me.

"I'm not just the school nurse," she explained. "I'm also a coach. And you've got more raw talent than I've ever seen before!"

So that's how I ended up at cross-country practice after school.

I know. I'm totally not the athletic type. But running is as good a hobby as any, I guess, to get my mind off the fact that my best friend hates me. It's definitely better than wallowing alone in my room every afternoon.

Plus, it was kind of nice to be needed, to tell you the truth.

"Ladies," announced Coach Fleet, when I met up with her at the track, "welcome Jessica Darling to the Pineville Junior High cross-country team!"

The Pineville Junior High cross-country team had

exactly four girls on it. Two of them were the Sampson twins. Everyone in school knows the Sampson twins. The other two girls I didn't recognize at all. The seventh grader who'd later introduce herself as Molly was a tiny but tough tomboy from Woodbeach Elementary. The eighth grader was Padma, who was experiencing major culture shock because her family had just moved to the crowded gridlock of New Jersey from the wide-open spaces of North Dakota.

All four girls looked at me skeptically.

"Really?" they asked.

"Really!" Coach Fleet said. "Now we're officially a team!"

Then Coach Fleet, the Sampson twins, Molly, and Padma jumped up and down and back-slapped and high-fived like I'd just won a gold medal.

"We had to forfeit every meet!" said Shandi, the Sampson twin with silver beads in her braids.

"Now we can actually compete!" said Shauna, the Sampson twin with gold beads in her braids.

Inspired by their unintentional rhyme, Padma started rapping.

"Used to be we hadda forfeit every meet/Now with J.D. we gonna compete!"

I must have looked confused because Coach Fleet explained how a cross-country team isn't an official team unless it has a minimum of five runners.

"And you make us five!" said the Sampson twins.

As we warmed up with a series of stretches, Coach Fleet explained that too many girls go out for the more glamorous after-school activities like CHEER TEAM!!! Or sports that actually attract fans like soccer or field hockey. With one and a half miles to cover in a race, it's kind of hard for cross-country runners to keep in view of spectators, unless the spectators are running alongside you, in which case the spectators would just be *on* the cross-country team instead of rooting for it.

Anyway, Coach Fleet was eager to see what kind of shape I was in. So she timed me and the rest of the team as we ran a mile and a half around the track. Six laps. The Sampson twins took off together and never looked back. I only saw the backs of their PJHS T-shirts. Molly started out with them for the first lap and a half or so, then fell back. I passed her on the third lap. Padma never tried to run any pace but her own. She started and finished behind me but just ahead of Molly.

I kind of surprised myself—and my teammates—by how easily I was able to complete the six laps. Don't get me wrong, I was tired and out of breath when I finished, but I didn't, like, collapse in a heap. The Sampson twins finished about three-quarters of a lap ahead of me. Padma and Molly finished about three-quarters of a lap behind.

No one talked as we cooled down. And in that quiet, I got paranoid. What if Molly and Padma were mad at me for running faster than they did?

Then Padma started rapping.

"J.D. got herself some crazy fast feet/Thank you, thank you, thank you, Coach Fleet!"

Her lyrics needed some work, but I appreciated the message anyway. Molly just smiled and nodded. She wasn't much of a talker.

"How long have you been running?" Shandi asked as she bent over to stretch her legs.

"Um." I recalled my time on the clock: 10:58. "About eleven minutes, I guess."

"Did you hear that?" Shandi asked.

"I did!" Shauna answered.

"Eleven minutes!" exclaimed the Sampson twins.

Then they burst into rapid-fire laughter: h-h-h-h-h-h-h-HA! They laughed fast, they talked fast, they ran fast. Everything the Sampson sisters did was fast. They were so fast that they frequently overlapped each other's sentences, as if the one sister wasn't expressing herself fast enough.

"What I meant was…" began Shandi.

"How long have you *trained*…" middled Shauna.

"…to be a runner?" ended the twins together.

It took some getting used to.

"Eleven minutes," I repeated.

The Sampson twins laughed again—h-h-h-h-h-h-h-HA!—then good-naturedly punched me in the shoulders. Shandi picked the right. Shauna the left.

"That's funny," they said.

"I like this girl," Shandi said.

"Me too," Shauna said.

"Welcome to the team," they said.

This was a very big deal because the Samspon twins are kind of famous around school because they're athletic and smart and pretty. And there's two of them. They're also lean and strong and graceful and could be star athletes in just about any sport, so nobody understands why they're on the girls' cross-country team. Though the boys' team never has a problem with its numbers, it's definitely the least popular sport among girls at Pineville Junior High.

By the end of that first practice, I think I already understood why the Sampson twins chose to be on the cross-country team: They love to run. And they're natural leaders who don't like—or need—to follow. For them, it's just that simple.

I wish it were that simple for me. Maybe someday it will be.

Chapter Twenty-Three

I've been practicing with the cross-country team every day after school for the past two weeks. I'm not close to catching up with the Sampson twins, but Coach Fleet is thrilled by my swift progress and so am I. Our team hasn't won any meets yet, but we're all in agreement that it's better to have a shot at winning than not having a shot at all. And despite our 0–4 record, it's an improvement over staying home and feeling sorry for myself and the mess I've made of seventh grade so far.

My parents have come to every meet to cheer me on. At the end of my first race, Padma heard Dad congratulate my fourth-place finish by my nickname. Inevitably, she started rapping, *"Yo, yo, yo, yo! Notso! Notso! Go, go, go, go! Notso! Notso!"* Ever since then, the Sampson twins call out "Yo,

Notso!" whenever they see me in the halls. This recognition by two of the coolest eighth graders impresses all the girls at my lunch table except Manda because she doesn't respond very well when anyone gets more attention than she does.

Actually, now that I'm on the cross-country team and I'm not in fear of failing Woodshop anymore, my friends are really the only sore spot in my life at the moment. (Other than my shins, which are so tired and achy from running up and down the bleachers and are currently slathered in a mentholated soothing balm that smells like cough drops, Christmas-tree air fresheners, and cat pee. But that's not what I meant by *sore spot* and I'm probably babbling parenthetically because my friends are a really awkward subject right now and I'm not sure how to begin. I guess I could start by closing these parentheses and moving on.)

Okay. Moving on.

So. My friends. The problem with my friends is even more complicated than my best friend hating me. Even my friends who don't hate me are causing drama. Most of the time at least one of us in the group is annoying the fecal matter out of someone else in the group. (Confession: I've noticed that Miss Orden gives me bonus points on my essays when I swap regular words with fancy thesaurus substitutions. That's why I used *fecal matter* instead of *crap*. Miss Orden isn't grading this story, but my Nerd Self couldn't stop my Trying to Be Normal Self. This happens a lot.) I don't feel guilty about saying this because I am equal parts irritat*ed* and irritat*ing*.

Take today's lunch, for example.

"Jessica," said Manda, "you're annoying the fecal matter out of me."

Only when Manda said it, she said *crap*.

Why was Manda so annoyed with me? I'd forgotten to wear the school colors—red, white, and blue—in honor of Pineville Junior High Spirit Day. Quite frankly, after I retired as mascot, I'd put all displays of school spirit behind me. And besides, I wasn't the only one who'd forgotten. Sara showed up for school in a pink polo and blue denim skirt. Why wasn't Manda hassling her?

"She's co-founder of the Spirit Squad," I said, gesturing toward Sara. "Not me."

That's when Manda turned to Hope for backup.

"You're the artist," Manda said to Hope. "Please explain to Jessica what happens when you combine red and white."

Without looking up from her doodles, Hope said, "Red and white make pink."

Manda turned to Sara.

"Sara, what color is your shirt?"

Sara frowned like this was a trick question and there

was no way she was going to answer it without being totally humiliated. Like, what if today was the day Sara discovered that her pink is everyone else's green?

"Pink?"

"Pink," Manda said with a curt nod.

And I swear Sara looked triumphant, as if she'd just discovered the solution to global warming. (Actually, she'd be crushed if she ended global warming. Global warming, she believes, is good for her tan. She'd be like, "You can have my Nobel Prize! I need to get back to the fake and bake!")

Anyway, Manda grabbed the hem of my T-shirt.

"And what color is your shirt, Jess?" Manda pressed. "It's not pink. Or red. Or white, is it?"

She stood there, hands on hips, waiting for me to deny this charge I couldn't deny. Recently I've decided that I actually like some of Bethany's old T-shirts. I keep wearing them even though I've come to realize that by Manda's definition, *interesting* means *ick*. Anyway, the Beatles shirt I was wearing at the time was black. It wasn't pink or red or white or any other color but what it was. Black.

"Actually," Hope said, tossing her notebook aside. "Jess's shirt is pink. And red. And white."

Manda and Sara both "whatevered" her.

And then Hope surprised us all. Especially me.

"Light is made up of all the colors of the spectrum.

When light hits an object, it can be absorbed, reflected, or it can shine right through." Hope took a breath before continuing. "Black is the absence of any reflected light, but it absorbs all the colors of the spectrum including pink. And red. *And* white."

"Omigod! Nerd alert! Shut up!" shouted Sara.

I happen to appreciate that Hope also uses bonus-point vocabulary words like *spectrum*. But I have a feeling she doesn't have to cheat with a thesaurus like I do.

Manda just huffed for a few seconds. Then she whipped out her wand and applied gloss to her lips, even though as far as I could tell they had already achieved maximum luster. (*Maximum luster* is thesaurus for *shiny*.) Then she huffed some more.

"Puh-leeze," she replied at last. "Anyone who can't remember something as simple as wearing school colors on Spirit Day has cranio-rectal syndrome."

Only Manda didn't say "has cranio-rectal syndrome." She said "has her head up her butt." And then she decided she'd had enough of me. It was time to flirt with Scotty Glazer, the only seventh-grade football player skilled enough to start with the eighth graders, which makes him cool enough to sit with them at lunch.

"Come on, Sara and Hope, let's show the team our spirit!"

Hope didn't get up right away. As we sat alone together, I noticed that she was wearing a black-and-white-striped T-shirt under her overalls.

"You never wear red, white, and blue on Spirit Day," I said to Hope.

Suddenly and without warning, a ball of crazy boy energy came crashing down beside Hope. It was Aleck! From Woodshop! I was surprised for two reasons: (1) Aleck had Language Arts seventh period and wasn't supposed to be here. (2) Aleck had been kind of distant with me ever since I retired Mighty the Seagull, as if that secret was the only reason he had bothered talking to me at all.

"Hey, Hope!" he said. "How's it going?"

Hope kind of half smiled, half winced.

"Uh. Okay. My friend Jessica and I were just discussing the lameness of Spirit Day. Have you guys met?"

I tried to hide the shock on my face. Hope and Aleck knew each other?

Aleck half smiled and said, "No. I've never met *Jessica*." He put special emphasis on my real name. "Have I?"

"No," I replied. "I guess you haven't."

Then he turned back to Hope.

"You're a conscientious objector to Spirit Day for follicular reasons," he said, pulling one of Hope's curls, then releasing it like a spring. "Like me."

It was all happening so fast that I barely had time to process what had just happened. *Conscientious WHAT? Follicular HUH?*

"See ya in Woodshop," he said with a wave, *"Jessica!"*

And then he sped off to the corner of the cafeteria where all the detention kids hang out.

I just kind of stared at Hope like, *WHAT JUST HAPPENED?*

"We're both redheads," she tried to explain. "Our hair clashes with the school colors big-time."

"Not that," I said. "I mean, you know Aleck, too?"

"Alec? His name isn't Alec."

"Oh! I know! But that's what our Woodshop teacher calls him. As in Smart Aleck. Or in his case, Dumb Aleck."

I turned around in my seat just in time to see Dumb Aleck balancing an open carton of milk on the tip of his nose. Straw and all.

"That's Marcus Flutie," Hope said simply. "We went to the same elementary school. He's friends with my older brother."

And that's when the carton of milk came crashing to the floor, splashing all over everyone who had a first-row seat to Aleck's—I mean, Marcus Flutie's—show of stupidity. They were too busy cracking up to care. For someone with such an impressive vocabulary, Marcus Flutie is an idiot. But I didn't settle for *idiot.*

"Well," I said, pausing dramatically. "He's terminally bizarre."

Terminally bizarre is a new phrase I'm trying out. I mean, if Manda could make and break *mondo*, why can't I create a new buzzword? But Hope just kinda shrugged when I said it.

Hmm. I'm not confident *terminally bizarre* will catch on.

I was about to ask Hope about her older brother—how old was he and what was he like and did he ever TOTALLY MESS WITH HER HEAD?—when Manda called over to her from the jocks' table. She was rubbing Burke Roy's bicep.

"Come here, Hope!" Manda commanded. "Burke here wants a Pineville Chicken tattoo and we need you to sketch it for him!"

Maybe Hope mouthed, "Seagull." I can't say for sure. I was too busy noticing that Manda was flirting with the boy everyone knew was supposed to officially ask out Bridget any second now. Even from across the room I could see Bridget's face had turned as red as the *P* on her PJHS CHEER TEAM!!! uniform. She had obviously noticed, too.

"Come onnnnnn, Hooooope."

Hope looked back and forth between Bridget and Manda/Burke. She wore an expression of weary resignation, then sighed heavily before standing up.

"Duty calls."

She was a half step away from the table when she turned around.

"You're so lucky you get to escape to Woodshop," she said. "I'm still mad at the guidance department for not switching me to Visual Arts. You have no idea how much I hate being in the middle of all this drama in Home Ec."

Oh, that's where Hope was wrong. I had an excellent idea of how much she hated being stuck in the middle. I've been stuck in the middle ever since I started seventh grade. Maybe that's why some junior highs are called middle schools.

Anyway, it was clear that Hope didn't want to go over there as much as I didn't want to go over there. What a relief that Manda didn't call for me. Because I don't think I could have lived with myself if I had gotten up, too, just to make good on IT List #4: Stick with the IT clique.

And while I'm being honest, I guess I should say this: I had looked forward to "meeting" Marcus Flutie in Woodshop today. But he must have cut class because he never showed up. I felt like such a foolish girlie-girl for being disappointed by his absence.

I don't want to feel that way again.

And that, to me, is reason enough to skip IT List #3: Pick your first boyfriend wisely.

Chapter Twenty-Four

September turned into October and I'VE GOT BIG NEWS.

The first bit of big news is that Bridget and I are talking to each other again.

I was the one who initiated the reconciliation by showing up at her house uninvited with sugary cereal and soda. Everyone in school knew that Burke had finally asked out Bridget and they were officially a couple. I figured that if she ever really believed that I had a thing for him—which, for the record, I never did—that she would be over it by now because she got him and I didn't, which is totally fine because I never wanted him anyway.

"Hey," I said when she came to the front door.

She was wearing her PJHS CHEER TEAM!!! uniform. There'd been a football game that afternoon. Somehow, even without the unique entertainment provided by Mighty the Seagull, the team managed to draw a crowd. Even if their 0–5 record was hardly anything to cheer about.

"Hey," she said.

And then I just stared at her faded welcome mat because I didn't know what to say next.

"I'm not supposed to eat that stuff," Bridget said. "If I want to fit into my uniform."

Then she actually pinched the waistline of her cheer skirt. Ack. Was fear of junk food yet another thing Bridget had in common with my sister and mother?

"Oh" was all I could say.

It was so awkward. So, so awkward. Until—suddenly— it wasn't anymore.

Bridget grabbed the box out of my hand and hugged it to the PJHS logo on her chest.

"But I don't care because I'm starving!"

She plopped herself down on the front step and I just kind of stood there for a moment, unsure of whether she wanted the box to herself or what. Then she brushed away some leaves and gestured for me to sit down beside her.

"Come on, Jess," she said, "I know you're starving, too! You must run, like, a bazillion miles at practice every day!"

Someone else must have told her I was on the cross-country team because I hadn't. It's possible she'd seen me running all around the school while she was at CHEER TEAM!!! practice. Maybe she couldn't help but notice me even when she was mad at me.

I sat down next to her. We opened our sodas and toasted with plastic bottles.

"CHEERS!!!"

I shouted it like Bridget had on our last junk-food picnic.

Bridget's eyes lit up. Then she shouted right back at me. "RACES!!!"

I was looking at her like, *Wha...?* when—duh!—I got it. *She* cheers. *I* race. We should celebrate both.

We didn't apologize to each other. We didn't talk about what happened between us because I don't think either of us understood what had happened between us. Avoiding that awkward conversation was fine with me because my best friend was talking to me again. The only downside to avoiding the awkwardness was how it could be interpreted as a sign that we weren't really best friends anymore.

Perhaps my changing friendship with Bridget wasn't an upside or a downside but a ... *middle*side?

"I think the CHEER TEAM!!! should cheer for cross-country and other sports besides football," Bridget said when we got to the bottom of the box. All that was left was a squinch of sugary cereal dust.

"Really?" I asked as she picked up the box and the bottles and stood up.

"Our football team, well…" She paused and looked around for eavesdroppers. "It kinda sucks."

I feigned horror. "Bridget! I could have your pom-poms revoked for such talk!"

"Don't tell Burke I said so, but it's true!" She was laughing harder than I'd heard her laugh in a long time. It was so great to hear her laugh like that, a laugh I've heard a bazillion times. "They've got the worst record in the whole school!"

I promised I wouldn't say anything to Burke or anyone else.

"Your secret is safe with me."

As I jogged back across the street to my house, I thought about how Bridget was probably the only person in the whole school who knew that the PJHS girls' cross-country team had ended its losing streak.

Yes! This is my second bit of big news! We won our first meet today!

We all delivered our personal bests. I was only fifteen seconds behind the Sampson twins, which was exciting because I'd never finished that close to them before! And it was even more exciting to scream for Padma and Molly and give them the boosts they needed to pass the competition in the final one hundred yards of the course.

"You worked together as a team," Coach Fleet said with tears in her eyes, "and you won together as a team!"

It was awesome. Now I kind of understand why sports are such a big thing.

And both parents were superproud of me, but my dad was particularly impressed.

"Who knew there was a jock inside you?" he joked, throwing a towel over my head.

Who knew? Not me, that's for sure.

My parents dropped me off at home so I could shower while they picked up paperwork (Mom) and a pizza (Dad).

With both of them out of the house, I should have expected a visitor.

"Heeeeey, sis!"

Yep. That's when my sister decided to show up for the first time since the last time I saw her. You know, when she told me I'd made the CHEER TEAM!!! and I lied to her about liking Burke Roy, which led to all the awkwardness with Bridget we couldn't talk about.

Honestly? I didn't want to talk about it with Bethany either. Besides, she appeared to be in no condition to have such a heart-to-heart anyway. Despite her cheery greeting, Bethany was downright frazzled. I mean, she had left the sorority house without applying eyeliner.

I answered her question before she even asked it.

"I have it!"

"You have it."

"The award letter from school! It arrived."

"WHERE IS IT?"

I told her I'd put it in her top drawer. Now, I'm pretty fast, but my sister was even faster. She'd already torn open the envelope when I crossed the threshold to her room. I expected her face to be flushed with excitement or that she'd be doing a victory dance around the room. Instead, her face was green and she clutched her stomach like she was about to barf.

"It's official," she said, dropping the letter to the floor. "My life's a mess!"

"What? I don't...understand."

Something was very, very wrong here.

I cautiously bent over to pick up the letter. It was addressed to my parents and basically said this: Your daughter is failing out of school. And you owe us money.

"Whoa! What kind of award is this?"

I was obviously still confused.

"It's not an award! I lied about the award!"

The truth still hadn't sunk in yet. I reread the letter.

"You're failing your classes?"

"I'm failing LIFE."

And that's when my popular, pretty, and perfect older sister totally and completely lost it.

"I'm on academic PROBATION and PROHIBITED from fulfilling my duties as CHEER CHAIR for my SORORITY and my BOYFRIEND BROKE UP WITH ME and I can't BORROW HIS CAR anymore to get to my STUPID JOB selling clothes at CHIC BOUTIQUE that expects me to wear only CHIC BOUTIQUE BRANDS even though they're only paying me, like, BARELY ABOVE MINIMUM WAGE and I've MAXED OUT my credit cards BUYING CHIC BOUTIQUE BRANDS that I was supposed to use to buy BOOKS for all the CLASSES I'm FAILING."

I edited all the sobs and snorts and other scary noises that came out of my sister throughout this monologue. Why add insult to injury? She was breathing really hard at the end of this rant, like I do after Coach makes us run repeats up and down Killer Hill at cross-country practice.

I really don't have an opinion on Bethany's breakup because I know nothing about boyfriend-and-girlfriend business. But it seems to me that Bethany liked the boyfriend's car more than the actual boyfriend and she'll get over her heartbreak soon enough.

As for everything else, I could have said something like, "Hey, if you'd spent your money on books and not clothes, gone to class instead of shopping, put in more time as a student and less time as sorority cheer chair—whatever that even *is*—then, I don't know, maybe you wouldn't be in this situation."

Then I remembered what Mr. Pudel said to Aleck— I mean, Marcus Flutie…oh, you know who I'm talking about!—about his "epic" toothpick: *Just because you* can *do something doesn't mean you* should.

So I didn't say any of that. But I didn't know what to say or do so I did something I can't ever remember doing before.

I hugged her.

And Bethany cried into my shoulder for a very long time. I didn't even mind that she was getting my cross-country uniform all slobbery.

After who knows how long, she finally let go of me. She wiped her eyes and said, "I needed that." Followed by, "I'm soooooo sorry." And another hug.

"Oh, that's okay," I said, patting her back. "It's just a little snot. My uniform was already all gross and sweaty anyway."

"Not the snot!" Bethany laughed, reeling back. "I'm sorry about the IT List. I should have never given it to you."

And then I finally posed the question I'd wanted to ask ever since my sister showed up on the last day of summer before seventh grade TO MESS WITH MY HEAD.

"Why *did* you give it to me?" I asked. "I mean, you never showed that much interest in me before. Why now?"

My sister lowered her gaze before replying.

"I thought it was to help you," she said quietly. "But now I think I gave it to you to help myself."

And then I gave her this look like I totally understood what she was talking about when I absolutely did not understand what she was talking about. My actress face must not have been too convincing because she went on.

"Here's the thing, Jessie. The last time I had it all figured out was back in junior high. I had all the answers to everything! And now it's like I don't have the answers to anything! I guess I wanted to recapture that all-knowingness...."

Her voice trailed off.

"Through me?" I asked.

She nodded grimly. "And I couldn't even do *that* right! The IT List totally backfired and now you're an even bigger loser than I am! You're still wearing those grungy T-shirts! Sherri told me you quit the CHEER TEAM!!! No wonder you don't have a boyfriend yet and can't get into the IT clique!"

I was about to pat her back again in sympathetic agreement when I stopped myself short.

Wait.

Hold on a second.

How am I an even bigger loser than she is?

I'm not a loser! Okay, so I'm not a fashion diva cheerleader with the hottest boyfriend and the coolest clique. I'm not the most popular, the prettiest, or anywhere near achieving perfection. And despite my total failure to make good on any of Bethany's rules, and the fact that my best friend was maybe not my best friend anymore, I'm way more happy than not happy about seventh grade so far. Doesn't that satisfaction count for something? If not *everything*?

Bethany's eyes were all wide and weepy, so I knew I had to speak up. And fast. I don't know how much more mucus my shirt could absorb.

"Bethany, the IT List *totally* worked!"

My sister rolled her eyes. "Jessie! I may be failing all my classes, but I've made it to enough Image Marketing and Management classes to know that you are trying to put a positive spin on things!"

"I'm not!" I argued. "I swear! If it hadn't been for the IT List I wouldn't be who I am right now!"

My sister paused before asking, "And who are you right now?"

I thought about it for a second. And in the silence I flashed back:

Mr. Pudel: *Whooooo are you? Doot doot. Doot doot.*

The pep rally crowd: *Whooooo are yooooooou?*

My ex-ex–best friend: *I don't know who you are anymore.*

Who am I? I'm Jessica Darling, seventh grader at Pineville Junior High School. Retired mascot. Up-and-coming cross-country star. Future I-don't-know-what.

"Jessie?" My sister was still waiting for an answer.

"I'm still figuring out who I am," I said, "but I'm happy."

Chapter Twenty-Five
(Bonus!)

It would have been awesome to stop right there, huh? But the truth is, life never ties itself up with a sweet little ending like that.

Because after that little epiphany my mom came home all pleased with herself about closing a deal on a pricy property and my dad came home with pizza and I promised Bethany I wouldn't say anything about the failing-out-of-school letter and convinced her to stay and eat with us because—duh!—FREE FOOD and she's broke and it would be nice for all of us to be a family for a while.

"All together again!" My mother seriously looked like she was about to cry.

My dad raised his water glass. "To my darling Darlings!"

And even though it was totally corny, Bethany and I—his darling Darlings—toasted him right back.

So we all ate pizza together; even my mom ate a slice along with her salad, which is, like, unheard of. My parents were already in such great moods and so happy to actually see Bethany in person that they seemed to totally forget about how much she's been stressing them out lately, which was good because they have no clue just how much *more* she's going to stress them out with her news of failing out of school. Whenever she decides to break that news, that is. She didn't tell them then because my parents were too busy asking all about *me* and *my life*, and I could tell that Bethany was relieved to have all eyes focused on someone else for a change.

Anyway, so I talked about how I'm catching up to the Sampson twins and how I'm not worried about failing Woodshop anymore and positive stuff like that. Eventually my parents went to the kitchen to clean up, and I got around to telling Bethany how I was still friends with Bridget, but I wasn't sure if we were *best* friends anymore because her new best friend might be our old best friend, Dori, and how that left me with my G&T friends, Hope, Manda, and Sara, and how I wasn't sure I even liked Manda or Sara, but they kind of came as a package with Hope because they all came from the same elementary school and how it's funny that

I like Hope a lot now even though I didn't like her when I first met her and...ACK.

Double ACK.

"Is it impossible for old elementary-school friends and new junior-high friends to all get along as just, you know, *friends*?"

"That can definitely be tough in seventh grade," Bethany said, blotting her pizza grease with a paper towel. "I actually have something—"

Then she stopped herself and took a huge bite out of her slice as if to shut herself up.

"What?" I was suddenly dying to hear what she obviously didn't want to say.

And then she said something that sounded like "nutter illest," and I said "what?" and she said "nutter illest" again, which I have since decided would totally be my rapper name if I ever took up Padma's offer to join her crew. YO! NUTTER ILLEST IN DA HOUSE.

But I digress.

Bethany swallowed, took a sip of diet soda, then answered in a low voice.

"Another IT List."

"Another IT List? How many did you make?"

Bethany smiled cryptically. "More than one."

"What's the next one called?"

Bethany looked behind her to make sure our parents were still busy in the kitchen. Then she leaned in and whispered.

"IT List Number Two: The Guaranteed Guide to Friends, Foes & Faux Friends."

WHAT? With all the tension between my old friends and my new friends that only sounded like THE EXACT THING I NEEDED.

"Where is it? Can I see it?"

Bethany's smile faded. "You really want to see it?"

I could hardly blame Bethany's reservation. The way she saw it, I failed miserably at making good on IT List #1. But I meant what I said earlier about how I wouldn't be who I am right now if she hadn't MESSED WITH MY HEAD. Bethany's "wisdom" forced me outside my comfort zone in a good way. I discovered parts of myself—runner, spoon maker, secret keeper—that I maybe wouldn't have found otherwise. For me, being popular, pretty, and perfect wasn't the point anymore. I don't think it ever really was. I just wanted to make it through the rest of junior high as me.

Whoever I am.

As bizarre as it sounded, my sister's IT List may be just the thing to help me achieve ultimate me-ness. In my totally screwed-up way, of course.

"Are you sure you want to see it?" Bethany repeated. "After what happened last time?"

"Are you kidding?" I sprung from my chair like a sprinter out of the starting blocks. "I want to see it *because* of what happened last time!"

And I can't wait to find out what will happen to me next.

Turn the page for a sneak peek!

Coming September 2014

Chapter One

Is it impossible for old elementary-school friends and new junior-high friends to all get along as just, you know, *friends*?

Good or bad, that's what I'm about to find out.

Lately my friends have been stirring up more drama than I can handle. This is really saying something because my first month of seventh grade was a doozy. Let's see. I went out for the CHEER TEAM!!! and face-planted with a *SPLAT!* when I tried—and failed—to do a simple cart-wheel. DRAMA. I nearly lost a finger making an ugly spoon in Woodshop—a class I'M NOT SUPPOSED TO BE IN taught by a singing giant straight out of Harry Potter. More DRAMA. And how could I forget the time I dressed up as Mighty the Seagull—the Official Pineville Junior

High School Mascot—and shook my red-white-and-blue-feathered booty in front of the entire school? Everyone thought I was a crazy chicken. Well, except a ginormous lovesick goose who mistook me for his new girlfriend and chased me all over the football field until I smashed beak-first into the goalpost.

DRAMA. DRAMA. And more DRAMA.

All of which could be traced back to the IT List my big sister gave me the day before the start of seventh grade.

My sister, Bethany, isn't exactly rocking her fifth year of college—um, especially since she failed all her classes and may not *technically* be a student anymore—but she ruled school when she was my age. She was always the center of attention and never had a shortage of friends and boyfriends. Her classmates considered her such an expert on all things awesome that they persuaded her to put that wisdom into writing "Bethany Darling's IT List: The Guaranteed Guide to Popularity, Prettiness & Perfection." No big sister was more qualified to share secrets of social success. And no little sister was less qualified to follow them.

And yet tonight at dinner when I happened to mention that I was having some issues with my friends—okay, I was ranting about how they were totally driving me crazy—Bethany casually let it slip that she had *another* IT List that could solve all my girl drama.

And I was like, "WAIT. WHAT? WHOA! I MUST HAVE THAT NEXT LIST!"

"You're *sure* you want it?" Bethany asked skeptically. "After what happened last time?"

Or, rather, after what *didn't* happen. Despite the "Guaranteed" promise in the title, I haven't become popular, pretty, or anywhere near perfect. From Bethany's point of view, I'd taken all the right advice in all the wrong directions.

I, however, saw it differently.

"Are you kidding?" I replied. "I want to see it *because* of what happened last time."

A slow smile spread across Bethany's face.

"Okay," she said assertively. "Let me get it. It's in my bedroom."

Bethany excused herself from the dining room, and I could hardly contain myself in her absence. See, here's the thing about DRAMA: As painful as it can be sometimes, it certainly makes life more interesting. When I think about what seventh grade would have been like without the first IT List, I get kind of drowsy, and the next thing I know I'm ZZZZZZ.

In other words: BORING.

A BAZILLION MINUTES LATER, Bethany breezed back in with an envelope in her hand. The second IT List!

"Are you suuuure you're in?" she asked teasingly.

"I'm in!" I promised. "I'm *so* in."

"In *what*?" asked my parents in the way that only my parents can.

I hadn't even noticed that they had finished cleaning up in the kitchen and were lurking in the doorway. My mom and dad are expert lurkers.

"In..." I stammered. "In...um..."

My sister shot me a warning look. Bethany wants to keep the IT Lists just between us. Maybe she's waiting until I'm confidently perched at the tippy-top of the social ladder before taking credit as the mastermind behind my meteoric rise from Not to Hot. Perhaps she doesn't want our parents blaming her for any subsequent face-breaking visits to the nurse's office. Who knows what's happening underneath that mane of glossy blond hair? With a ten-year gap between us, Bethany and I have had few opportunities to bond over sister-to-sister stuff. I'm more than happy to comply with her rules if it means she won't go back to forgetting that I exist.

"She's in with the in crowd," my sister clarified for me. "The IT clique."

Mom's eyes lit up. Dad's eyebrows shot up.

"Really!" said Mom.

"Really?" asked Dad.

"Really," confirmed my sister.

I thought, *No, not really.*

Then I considered how I had two friends on the elite CHEER TEAM!!! and two more friends on the super-duper-exclusive Spirit Squad and thought again.

Well, sort of.

I've noticed the way other girls in our grade pass our lunch table and look at us with something like envy because we sit in a totally up-and-coming part of the cafeteria surrounded by Hots.

Maybe?

"If she isn't already," Bethany said as she handed over the envelope, "she will be."

Then she blew kisses at all of us, said her good-byes, and dashed out the door. Bethany loves dramatic entrances and exits. She excels at them.

"What did she give you, Jessie?"

Mom craned her neck to see for herself. I instinctively tucked the IT List into the pouch of my sweatshirt. I needed to be as overprotective as a mama kangaroo.

"I don't know," I lied. "I haven't opened it yet. Duh."

My mother pinched her lips, torn between coming down on me for being rude and kissing up to me to find out what was in the envelope. Curiosity won out.

"Well," she said with a slightly strained expression,

"don't you want to know what's inside? Aren't you going to open it?"

Of course I wanted to know what was inside. *Obviously*, I was going to open it. I was dying to read the IT List, but I make a point of never looking too eager about anything in front of my parents because they'd instantly get all suspicious that I'm up to something shady. Then they'd start asking ridiculous questions I don't want to answer that would inevitably put a damper if not a major delay on the very thing I'm excited about. So I had to pretend not to care too much about Bethany's envelope if I ever hoped to read it in all its wisdom tonight.

"Eh. It's probably nothing." I nonchalantly pulled the drawstring on my hoodie. "I'll open it later."

My strategy worked. Before long the intrigue of the envelope faded, and the Darling household was restored to its normal state of boringness.

"Have you finished your homework?" Mom asked.

"Have you *started* your homework?" Dad asked.

Woo-hoo! It was the out I'd been waiting for.

"No and no," I blurted. "Gotta go hit the books!"

I hung a DO NOT DISTURB. HOMEWORK IN PROGRESS sign on my bedroom door. I'm usually a very diligent student. I always get my homework done before I watch TV or gossip with my friends. However, Language Arts and Pre-

Algebra were not my priorities just then. After all, I already knew the difference between a preposition and a participle, a matrix and a mode. But could I make it through one more day of lunch-table drama without the IT List? No, only the IT List contained the life-changing advice I really needed to learn if I was going to survive junior high with friends by my side.

Or so I hoped.

Chapter Two

IT List 2
The Guaranteed Guide to Friends, Foes & Faux Friends

1. 1 BFF < 2 BFFs < 4 BFFs < 8 BFFs < INFINITY BFFs
2. Have fun with your enemies.
3. PARTY!!!
4. When all else fails: CANDY.
5. There is no I in CLIQUE.

That's it.

That's *IT*?

The document containing the secrets to a lifetime of stress-free friendships was written on the back of a glittery invitation to a slumber party that took place at the house of some girl named Julia almost ten years ago. That might sound strange, but the first IT List had been written in lip liner on the back of a ten-year-old Pineville Junior High CHEER TEAM!!! travel schedule.

And like its predecessor, IT List 2 left me with more questions than answers.

As they came to me:

1. How can I have MORE THAN ONE best friend forever, let alone INFINITY best friends forever if—by the very definition of the word *best*—there can be only ONE that is better than the rest, which is what makes that BFF the BEST?

2. Why would I want to have fun with my enemy? If my enemy is so awesome to be around, why are we enemies? Wouldn't we be friends?

3. Am I throwing the PARTY!!!? Or am I merely expected to get invited to and attend the PARTY!!!? Is it deeper than that? Like, do I need to go through junior high with a PARTY!!! attitude like the most popular 8th-Grade Hots, who bounce around the halls shouting "WOOOOOOOOOOOOT!" even when there doesn't seem to be anything worth celebrating?

4. Okay. This one makes sense to me. I love candy. I'd never underestimate the peacemaking properties of candy. Candy is good. The problem is, I've never seen

my sister actually eat anything even vaguely resembling candy, which makes me think that maybe I've got this all wrong.

5. But there *TOTALLY IS* an *I* in *clique*. Even when it's misspelled like "click," which is how I used to write it in elementary school because that's what the word *clique* sounds like. Not "clee-KAY" or "clee-KWAY," which is how you'd think it would be pronounced with that *q-u-e* arrangement and everything. And while on the subject of weird foreign spellings, here's an FYI: *Faux* rhymes with *foe*. I found this out the hard way when I once mispronounced *faux* so it sounded a little too close to another four-letter word, which made my mom threaten to wash my mouth out with soap.

So. Uh. Anyway. Where was I? Oh yeah. My sister had MESSED WITH MY HEAD. Again.

Even worse? I asked for it this time! I can only hope that the path to ultimate me-ness is more straightforward—and less mortifying—with this second IT List than it was with the first!